THE GIRLS
FROM CABIN SIX

KATIE, the born leader, loves the competition of Color War—and she plays to win!

TRINA, always the sensitive one, can't stand to see either side lose.

ERIN, much more interested in boys, thinks games are baby stuff.

SARAH, always eager to avoid exercise, would rather be eating than playing games.

MEGAN, the daydreamer, would rather lose herself in fantasy than win or lose a game.

Color War!

Marilyn Kaye

AN AVON  CAMELOT BOOK

CAMP SUNNYSIDE FRIENDS #3: COLOR WAR! is an original publi-
cation of Avon Books. This work has never before appeared in book form.

AVON BOOKS
A division of
The Hearst Corporation
105 Madison Avenue
New York, New York 10016

First Avon Camelot Printing: September 1989

CAMELOT TRADEMARK REG. U.S. PAT. OFF. AND IN OTHER COUNTRIES, MARCA
REGISTRADA, HECHO EN U.S.A.

Printed in the U.S.A.

OPM 10 9 8 7 6 5 4 3

For Kathy Charlap,
with thanks for sharing her color war experiences

Chapter 1

stupid

"It's almost time for dinner," Trina Sandburg announced to the campers in cabin six. She stood in front of the mirror, checking to make sure her white shorts were crisp and clean and her Camp Sunnyside tee shirt neatly tucked in.

Beyond her own reflection, she could see her cabin mates, and she shook her head in exasperation. "C'mon, you guys, we don't want to get demerits for being late again. Erin, you better wash your face."

The slender girl with the blonde-streaked hair rose languidly from her bed and joined Trina at the mirror. Gingerly, she touched the brown muddy-looking stuff that covered everything but her eyes. "The directions said to leave it on for fifteen minutes."

"But you've had that stuff on your face for half an hour!" Trina said.

"I figure if I leave it on twice as long, it will

1

work twice as well." She was speaking stiffly, as if she were trying to keep the dried cream from cracking.

From one of the upper bunks, Sarah Fine took her eyes off her book long enough to adjust her glasses and eye Erin curiously. "Why did you put that stuff on your face anyway?"

"For my complexion," Erin mumbled, barely moving her lips.

"There's nothing wrong with your complexion," Trina said. "It's just fine."

"It's fine now," Erin replied darkly. "But I'm almost twelve. And you know what that means."

Trina didn't. "What?"

"Acne!" And Erin shuddered as she said the dreaded word.

Trina rolled her eyes. Then she turned back to the others with her hands on her hips. "Wake up, Megan," she said sternly. The tiny girl with the red curls stared at her blankly. Megan's eyes were wide open, but Trina could tell from her expression that she was off on one of her usual daydreams.

Megan blinked, then grinned and hopped off her bed. "I'm ready," she said, attempting without much success to smooth her wrinkled tee shirt. "Anyone know what's for dinner? I'm hungry."

Above her, Sarah closed her book and climbed down the ladder. "I'm not."

Megan looked at her in surprise. "You're not hungry?"

2

"Nope." She paused. "I'm *starving.*"

"You're always starving," Erin noted as she went into the bathroom.

"Well, you would be too if the nutritionist had put you on a diet," Sarah called after her. "Hey, where's Katie?"

As if on cue, the cabin door burst open and Katie Dillon rushed in. "Sorry I'm late," she said breathlessly. "I was working in arts and crafts and I lost track of the time."

Trina gazed at her in amusement. "Were you painting by any chance?"

"How did you know?" Katie asked.

"Check out your tee shirt," Trina replied.

Katie looked down and groaned. "Oh no! And all my other ones are in the laundry!"

Trina strode briskly to her bed, and opened the drawer under it. "Here, I've got a clean one you can borrow."

"Thanks," Katie said gratefully.

"No problem," Trina said. "After all, what are best friends for?"

Suddenly, there was a scream from the bathroom. For a second, everyone froze. Then they all ran in.

Erin was standing at a sink, frantically splashing her face with water. "It won't come off!" she wailed. The brown mud was wet, but it was still stuck to her face.

"Good grief!" Katie exclaimed. "You look horrible!" And Megan started giggling, which only made Erin wail louder.

Trina took charge. "Calm down, Erin." She touched her face. The mask was hard as a rock. "We'll have to soak it off." She turned the hot water on and let it run until it was steaming. She filled the sink, and drenched a towel in the water.

"Hold still," she ordered Erin. Then, gently, she wrapped the towel around Erin's face. "Hold it there for a minute."

Erin's whimpers were muffled by the towel. The others stood around and watched her anxiously. "Should I get Carolyn?" Sarah asked.

Trina shook her head. "She's at a counselors' meeting. Besides, Erin will be okay." She checked her watch. "Okay, I think that's long enough." She pulled the towel from Erin's face. A lot of the brown gunk came with it, and Trina gently rubbed the rest off.

Erin looked in the mirror and moaned. "My face is red!"

"It'll fade," Trina assured her.

"How did you know what to do?" Katie asked Trina.

"It happened to my mother once. She put this mask on her face, and then she fell asleep. This was nothing compared to what I had to do to get the stuff off her face!" Trina smiled as she remembered that day. Her mother had always been a little scatterbrained, and sometimes Trina had to take care of *her*. She didn't mind, though. She'd

4

always been the responsible type, careful and cautious.

Now that the excitement was over, the girls went back into the main room. Katie pulled off her paint-splattered tee shirt and slipped on Trina's clean one.

"Try not to get into any food fights tonight, okay?" Trina asked.

Katie grinned. "Well, I promise not to start one. And if someone else does, I'll duck."

Trina grinned back at her. She was lucky to have a best friend like Katie at camp. In a way, they were opposites. People were always telling Trina she was too serious. Katie, on the other hand, was always getting into some kind of mischief. But she got Trina to take some risks and let her hair down. And Trina was sensible enough to keep Katie from getting out of hand. They made a good team.

Their counselor hurried into the cabin. "Are you girls ready for dinner? Let's go!"

Trina looked at Carolyn with interest. She looked sort of excited, like she knew something they didn't. Maybe they were having something special for dinner.

Sarah seemed to be having similar thoughts as the girls followed Carolyn out of the cabin and down the slope toward the dining hall. "Hope we're not getting spaghetti and meatballs tonight."

"But that's your favorite," Carolyn said.

"I know," Sarah said mournfully. "And that means I'll want seconds."

As they approached the dining hall, Trina noticed something unusual. "Hey, it looks dark inside."

Sure enough, as they entered the hall, they were greeted by pitch-black darkness. Trina could barely make out the figures of all the other campers feeling their way inside and around the tables. She could hear them, though. "Hey, what's going on?" "Did the fuse blow?" "Somebody get the lights!"

Finally, somebody did. And Trina, along with all the other campers, gasped. The dining hall walls were strung with blue and red streamers. Suspended from the ceiling there was a huge net which burst open. And what looked like hundreds of red and blue balloons floated down.

A whoop went up from the crowd as they all recognized the signal. "It's color war!" Katie screamed.

The whole place erupted in shrieks and cheers. As the counselors hustled the girls toward the lines to collect their trays, Katie grabbed Trina's arm. "I knew it would be any day now," she cried gleefully. "I've been waiting for this all summer!"

Trina smiled at her affectionately. Katie *loved* color wars. She was definitely into competition.

The others were excited too. "I hope we have a tennis series," Megan said, hopping up and down. "I'll bet I can beat any girl in this camp." She

6

sounded a little boastful, but Trina knew it was the truth. There was no one at Sunnyside who could give Megan a really intense game. Usually, she played with a great player from Eagle, the boys' camp across the lake.

Even Sarah, who had never been very involved in color wars before, was enthusiastic. "This will be the first year I can be in the swimming relay," she said happily. "I still have to work on my speed, but at least now I can kick and stroke at the same time."

Only Erin didn't look very enthusiastic. "Color wars," she murmured, brushing her hair back from her shoulders. "Baby stuff."

Trina looked at her with amusement. Erin always tried to act terribly sophisticated, as if all the activities at Sunnyside were just a little beneath her. But Trina had a feeling that once the war got started, Erin's competitive spirit would emerge.

But would Trina's? Trina had to admit she wasn't really the competitive type. She enjoyed the games and sports, but she could never feel that the other team was a rival. When she lost a game, it didn't break her heart. And when she won, she didn't get an incredible thrill. Sometimes, she felt so sorry for the person who lost that she couldn't even feel that good about winning.

The girls were still talking about the war when they gathered with their trays at their table. "Remember when we shaved the balloons?" Katie asked. "That was great!"

Sarah made a face. "All I remember is how everyone laughed at me."

Megan giggled. "That's because you jumped six feet in the air everytime a balloon popped. But you were great in the pie eating contest."

"I won't be great this year," Sarah warned her. "Cherry pies are not on my diet." She cocked her head to one side thoughtfully. "Maybe we could have a carrot eating contest instead."

Their conversation stopped abruptly as Ms. Winkle went up to the microphone at the front of the room. The camp director beamed at the girls. "I know you're all excited about color war, and you're anxious to get started. We've got lots of exciting events planned this year. But I want you all to listen carefully to what I have to say first."

The cabin six girls exchanged knowing looks. They really didn't have to listen. Ms. Winkle made the same speech every year.

"You must all remember that you're all Sunnyside girls, whether you're a red or a blue. And even though you'll be loyal to your color, your first loyalties are to Sunnyside. That means you're not going to do anything malicious to the opposing team members, play any nasty pranks, or do anything that would be contrary to our Sunnyside creed. Yes, color war is a competition, but here at Sunnyside it's a friendly competition, and it's all for fun. So keep that spirit, and we'll have a wonderful time. And now, about the team captains . . ."

Ears all over the room pricked up. Ms. Winkle paused dramatically before continuing. "Anyone wanting to run for team captain may announce this at breakfast tomorrow. And at dinner tomorrow evening, you can cast your ballot."

"When's breakout?" someone called.

Ms. Winkle smiled. "You'll find out when it's time for you to know." As she left the microphone, the conversation in the room rose to an unusually high level.

"What's breakout?" Carolyn asked.

Trina remembered that it was Carolyn's first summer as a camp counselor. "That's when we find out what team we're on."

"It's always done in a different way," Erin explained. "Like once, our old counselor, Nina, tied blue ribbons around our bedposts while we were sleeping."

"Cabin six has always been blue," Megan told Carolyn. "I don't know why, but it's always just worked out that way."

"I wonder who the blue captain will be," Sarah mused.

Katie leaned forward. "I'm thinking about running."

The others gazed at her in amazement. "But the captains are always the oldest kids," Erin pointed out.

Katie sniffed. "There's no rule that says you

9

have to be thirteen to be a color war captain. I think I could do just as good a job."

"I do too," Trina said. "You'd make a great captain."

"What do the captains do, exactly?" Carolyn asked.

"They choose the kids for the different events," Katie told her. "And help organize everything, and just generally be the leader. You have to have a lot of spirit and get your team to practice and all that."

"It's a lot of work," Erin reminded her. "I wouldn't want to do it."

Megan grinned. "If you were captain, Erin, we'd probably have contests for the best eye makeup."

"Do lots of girls run for captain?" Carolyn asked.

"Not that many," Trina told her. "Like Erin said, it's a lot of work, and most of the kids just want to have a good time during color war."

"I only want to run for captain if I have a chance of winning," Katie said. Trina nodded understandingly. Katie hated to lose anything.

"I think you've got a good chance," Trina told her. "Lots of kids think the thirteen year olds are too bossy."

"That's true," Katie said. "And the little kids don't know the older ones anyway. I'll bet if I was really friendly to them, they'd vote for me. Maybe I could bribe them with something."

"Katie!" Carolyn exclaimed. "That doesn't sound fair!"

Katie laughed. "All's fair in color war. You just wait and see!" Then her forehead puckered. "But what if I lose? I'd be so embarrassed."

Trina smiled. Katie definitely wanted this. It showed how different they were. Team captain wasn't a job *she'd* ever want. You might be a big camp hero if your team won, but if the team lost, you'd get the blame.

Katie would be willing to take that risk, but Trina wouldn't. It would be fun having Katie as team captain though. If the blues won, Trina would be so proud of her. And if they lost—well, Katie would still be her best friend, and Trina would be there to make her feel better.

"Go for it!" Trina said suddenly. "We'll all campaign for you. And I bet you'll win!"

Katie gave her a big, grateful smile. "Okay. I'll do it!"

Chapter 2

The next morning after breakfast, the entire dining hall fell silent as Ms. Winkle made an announcement. "Will all the girls who want to run for color war captain please come forward?"

All eyes were on the tables where the girls in cabins nine and ten were sitting. Four girls got up and started toward the front of the room. The others at their tables cheered and applauded.

But the eyes at the cabin six table were on Katie. Trina gave her a big smile and a thumbs-up sign. "C'mon, Katie," Megan urged.

With a flushed face and a fixed smile, Katie rose. Trina watched proudly as Katie marched up to the front of the dining hall and joined the line. Trina wanted to yell something like "Go, Katie," but she didn't want everyone staring at her. Luckily, Megan and Sarah had no problem with that.

"Yay, Katie!" they shrieked and began clapping

13

wildly with their hands in the air. And Trina joined in the applause.

The girls in line watched Katie approach with expressions that ranged from surprise to disapproval. And when Katie took her place next to Maura Kingsley, the older girl edged away as if Katie had a contagious disease.

Trina would have just about died if anyone ever looked at her like that. But Katie just ignored the stares and beamed at the campers. One by one the girls announced their names and their cabins, and as they did, there was more cheering. Katie went last, and she spoke loudly and clearly. "I'm Katie Dillon from cabin six."

Once again, the cabin six girls applauded, and then Ms. Winkle spoke. "Here are your candidates, girls. I'm sure you know them all, but you might like to spend the day getting to know them better before you vote."

Trina looked over the lineup. Besides Katie, she recognized the others though she didn't know them very well. The girls from cabins nine and ten stuck together, and didn't really have much to do with the younger kids at camp.

"Yuk, Maura Kingsley," Megan muttered, making a face. "I hope *she* doesn't win. What a snob."

"She is *not*," Erin argued. "She's just mature, that's all. And sophisticated."

Trina grinned. "You just like her because she's thirteen and you wish you were." Erin was always trying to hang out with the older girls. She considered herself much more mature than the other girls in cabin six.

Erin sniffed. "Well, I like her. And I wouldn't even mind being on her team."

The others stared at her in consternation. "If Katie doesn't win," Erin added hastily.

"*I* wouldn't want to be on her team," Sarah stated firmly. "But I wouldn't mind if she ended up being captain of the reds." Her eyes narrowed. "Then I'd feel like I had a real enemy to battle."

"Now, Sarah," Carolyn said reprovingly. "Remember what Ms. Winkle said. This is supposed to be a friendly competition. And besides, you don't know for sure that you're going to end up on the blue team."

"But we've always been blues," Megan pointed out.

"That's just a coincidence," Carolyn said.

"I really don't care if we're reds or blues," Sarah said. "As long as Maura's on the other side."

Trina could understand her feelings. Maura had been particularly nasty to Sarah when she was learning how to swim. She'd made cutting remarks about the big splash Sarah made when her chubby body hit the water, and she'd really hurt Sarah's feelings.

Katie returned to the table looking excited. "How was I? Could you hear me when I said my name?"

15

"Absolutely," Carolyn said. "You sounded very confident."

"I've just got to win," Katie said fervently. "I know I could make this the best color war ever!"

Trina believed her. Katie had more camp spirit than anyone. "We'll all help you," she promised. "But we've only got today to campaign. What should we do?"

"We could pool our ice cream coupons and hang out at the ice cream stand," Megan suggested. "And we'd treat everyone to cones if they promise to vote for Katie."

"But then we wouldn't have any left for ourselves for the rest of the summer," Sarah said in dismay.

Erin eyed her sternly. "You're not supposed to eat ice cream anyway. You're on a diet, remember?"

"But I'm not going to be on a diet forever," Sarah protested.

Carolyn spoke up. "You guys are not going to bribe people with ice cream," she stated flatly. "That's not the proper way to win an election."

"What do you think we should do?" Katie asked.

"I think personal contact is the best idea," Carolyn told her. "Try to see as many kids as you can today, tell them why you're running and how you'll make this a great color war."

Just then an older girl appeared at their table. "Here," she said abruptly. She passed out strips of paper. Each one read "Vote for Maura for color war captain." Then she hurried to the next table.

Katie looked at the paper glumly. "How did she get this done so fast?"

"She's probably been planning to run ever since she got to camp," Trina said.

"We could make up some signs in arts and crafts," Sarah suggested.

Katie turned to Trina. "What do you think?"

Trina considered this. "I think Carolyn's right," she said finally. "Let's not waste time with signs and things like this." She crumpled Maura's flyer. "Among us, we can talk to every camper here today. We'll spread out. Megan can cover the tennis courts, Sarah can hit the stables, and so on." She paused thoughtfully. "I don't think we should bother with the older kids. They're probably committed to Maura or one of the other ones. But there's plenty of younger kids, and if we can get them on our side, Katie could definitely win."

Katie's eyes were shining. "That sounds great," she said happily. "Trina, you're so smart!"

"Let's go back to the cabin and organize this," Trina said, getting up. "That way we can make sure we cover the camp."

Sarah and Megan nodded in agreement and rose. With Carolyn and Katie, they started toward the exit. Only Erin remained seated for a moment, frowning slightly.

"What's the matter?" Trina asked. "Aren't you going to campaign with us?"

Slowly, Erin got up. "Yeah, I guess," she said, without much enthusiasm. "But I don't want to get Maura and those other girls mad at me."

Trina put her hands on her hips. "Look, Erin, I know you like hanging around with those girls. But your loyalty to cabin six comes first."

"I know, I know," Erin said sullenly. She sighed dramatically, and walked toward the exit. Watching her, Trina shook her head in annoyance. Erin was always sulking about one thing or another.

But even so, Trina knew she'd come through. Cabin six girls always stood together. They'd been together in the same cabin for three years, playing together, working together, standing up for one another. Occasionally they'd argue and fight, but in the end, their loyalties and friendships always overcame their differences.

And that was important to Trina. At home, there were only she and her mother since her parents got divorced earlier in the year. More than ever, she'd looked forward to camp this summer for the good feelings she got when she was with her friends in cabin six. And with Katie as color war captain, they'd get even closer, working together to win. They'd be more than a team—they'd be a family!

And with that happy thought, she hurried to catch up with the others.

Trina couldn't remember a time when she'd talked to so many people in one day. Basically, she was a little shy about striking up conversations with kids she didn't know. But today she forced herself to talk to girls she'd barely spoken to before.

In archery, she marched up to a younger girl who seemed to be having some trouble stringing her bow. "Let me help you with that," Trina said.

Gratefully, the girl handed over the bow.

"What's your name?" Trina asked conversationally as she untwisted the string.

"Linda. I'm in cabin four."

"I'm Trina, from cabin six." She couldn't think of any way to ask the next question gracefully, so she just plunged in. "Do you know who you're going to vote for to be color war captain?"

The younger girl shrugged. "I guess that girl with the long blonde hair, Alice. She looked nice. Actually, I don't know any of those girls. Who are you going to vote for?"

"Katie Dillon," Trina said. She handed back the bow. "I promise you, she's the best."

"Okay," the girl said. "I'll vote for her."

"Great! And maybe you could tell the other girls in cabin four, okay?"

"Sure," the girl said agreeably.

Trina beamed. This was easier than she had expected. She had a chance to do more campaigning later in arts and crafts. She wandered over to a table where some kids who looked about eight years old were sewing beads on leather belts. Trina figured they had to be first-timers at Sun-

19

nyside, and probably didn't know any of the girls running for captain.

"Anyone need any help?" she asked brightly.

Nobody responded. Trina tried again. "Are you guys excited about color war?"

One kid made a face. "I heard the captains never let the younger kids do the really good stuff."

Trina seized the opportunity. "Katie Dillon will," she said. "She wants everyone involved equally. If she wins, she'll let you kids do anything you want." She felt a little funny making this promise. After all, she didn't really know if Katie would do this!

And the girls looked at her doubtfully.

"Really," Trina insisted. "She'll be much more fair than those older girls would be. So vote for Katie, okay?"

By the time she left them, she felt pretty certain she had six more votes in the bag.

At dinner that evening, Trina couldn't take her eyes off the big box at the entrance. Throughout the meal, campers walked over to it and dropped ballots in.

Katie's eyes were glued to it too. "I wonder when Ms. Winkle will announce the winners."

"Probably at breakfast tomorrow," Carolyn said. Katie groaned.

"How am I going to wait that long?"

Trina patted her arm. "There's a camp fire tonight. That will take your mind off it for a while."

Katie looked skeptical. And then something caught her eye, and she frowned. "What's Erin doing?"

Trina turned to look. Erin was standing by the table where Maura and her friends were sitting. Even from a distance, Trina could tell she was laughing with them.

Megan's eyes widened with horror. "You don't think she voted for Maura, do you?"

"She wouldn't do that," Trina said, but even as she spoke, she wondered. The same thought was on everyone's mind. And as Erin returned to the cabin six table, their expressions must have warned her about their thoughts.

"Why are you all staring at me like that?" she demanded.

"Who did you vote for?" Sarah asked bluntly.

Carolyn quickly intervened. "Sarah, voting is supposed to be confidential. Erin doesn't have to tell you who she voted for."

Erin tossed her head and sat down. Everyone watched her as she picked up her fork and starting picking at her cake. At first, she ignored them. Then, finally, she put her fork down and leaned forward. "Okay, I'll tell you. I voted for Katie."

There was a general sigh of relief at the table. "Thanks," Katie said.

"But don't tell anyone, okay?" Erin added. "Because I told Maura I voted for her."

Sarah gasped. "You lied?"

"It's just a little white lie. What if she wins and I'm on her team? I need to be on her good side."

"But where's your sense of loyalty to Katie?" Trina asked.

Erin sighed. "Look, I voted for Katie. Isn't that enough?"

The others exchanged looks. Erin could be so impossible.

Carolyn got up. "Is everyone finished? I think we should go back to the cabin and do something quiet, like reading, before the camp fire."

Katie eyed the ballot box longingly, as if she wanted to rip it open and count the votes right then and there. But Trina poked her, and they got up to leave.

Back in the cabin, no one except Sarah was in a mood to settle down and read. Trina tried to get Katie involved in a game of Scrabble but it was no use. Katie just couldn't concentrate.

"I just had this awful thought," she said suddenly. "What if Maura gets captain of the blues and we're all on her team? Can you imagine how she'll treat us?"

"She'll let me do anything I want," Erin said loftily. "Then, if you guys are nice to me, I'll get her to let you do some good things too."

Sarah looked up from her book. "If I'm on Maura's team, I'll just flat out refuse to do anything. I won't even be in color war at all."

"But Sarah, you have to be in color war!" Megan exclaimed.

22

"Stop worrying," Trina ordered them. "There's no point in even discussing this until we know who's going to be captain. Now, c'mon, let's play Scrabble."

But it was no use. Everyone was just too excited to settle down and play a game. And finally, Carolyn emerged from her room and announced that it was time for the camp fire.

The fire was blazing by the time the girls arrived at the camp fire area. "Oh goody," Megan said, "we're having s'mores."

Sarah moaned when she saw the makings for the traditional camp fire treat—graham crackers, marshmallows, and chocolate bars. "I'm going to ask the nutritionist if I can have just one."

Trina smiled sympathetically. "But you can never have just one. That's why they call them s'mores—because you always want some more."

But before they could attack the food, the entire camp gathered in a big circle around the fire. And Ms. Winkle led them in singing the official camp song. By now, they'd sung this song a zillion times that summer. But with color war coming on, everyone seemed to be singing with a fresh enthusiasm.

"I'm a Sunnyside girl, with a Sunnyside smile,
And I spend my summers in Sunnyside style,
I have sunny, sunny times with my
    Sunnyside friends,
And I know I'll be sad when the summer ends,

23

But I'll always remember with joy and pride,
My sunny, sunny days at Sunnyside!"

"Where's Katie?" Trina asked. She looked around. Katie seemed to have disappeared in the crowd.

"Look!" Megan cried out. "What's that?"

Several counselors were pushing what looked like two gigantic cakes into the circle. As they got closer, Trina could see that they weren't really cakes at all, but two huge drumlike things—one swathed in blue paper, the other in red.

By now everyone was looking at them, and an excited murmur went through the crowd.

Ms. Winkle stood between the two drums. "May I have everyone's attention, please?" she called out. She didn't need to ask for it. Every camper had turned expectant eyes on her, and Trina could feel the electricity in the air.

"I would like to present . . ." She paused dramatically. "The color war captains!"

The tops of the drums burst open. Maura emerged from the red one. At the very same time, out of the blue one popped Katie.

The crowd exploded. Shrieks, screams, cheers, and yells filled the air. And for once, Trina didn't care if anyone looked at her. She was shrieking and screaming and cheering and yelling just as much as anyone. Maybe even more!

Chapter 3

rediculus

When the cabin six girls arrived at the swimming pool the next morning, Katie was immediately surrounded by well-wishers from other cabins. The air rang with cries of "congratulations" and "I hope I get on your team."

Trina watched Katie's pleasure with enormous satisfaction. She was enjoying this as much as Katie was. As her best friend, she felt like she shared the glory.

Darrell, the swimming coach, blew his whistle, and the commotion died down. "Okay, everyone in the water!"

The campers obliged, jumping or diving or sliding in, and then waited for further instructions.

"Now, I've been seeing a lot of sloppy kicking lately," Darrell announced. "You're getting lazy! I want everyone to find a place on the side, hold on, and start kicking. I'm going to be checking your form and your rhythm, and I want to see some serious work!"

Trina grabbed the edge of the pool and started kicking. Next to her, Katie was doing the same— but Trina could tell her mind wasn't on her legs.

"I still can't believe it," Katie said. "Me—color war captain! I'll bet I'm the first eleven-year-old color war captain in the history of Sunnyside!"

Trina agreed, but she didn't say anything. Darrell was above them on the landing. "Very good, Trina. Katie, you're kicking from the knees. Keep those legs straight! And stop talking!"

His criticism didn't seem to bother Katie at all. Trina wasn't surprised. Ever since the camp fire last night, Katie had been floating on a cloud. And nothing—not even a rebuke from their handsome swimming coach—was going to bring her back to earth.

As soon as he was out of earshot, Katie started talking again. "I had a great idea. Remember those stupid original skits we had to do last year?"

Trina remembered, and shuddered. Skits were her least favorite color war competition. She always got stage fright and forgot her lines. "We had a terrible skit. Nobody even laughed at the jokes."

"This year," Katie continued, "maybe each team could act out a story everyone knows. Like a fairy tale or a nursery rhyme. That could be hysterical! Can't you just picture Erin being Cinder-

26

ella? Or maybe she'd be better as a wicked stepsister!"

Trina lifted her head to make sure Darrell wasn't watching them. "Don't the team captains have to agree on all the rules for each activity?"

"Of course. Why?"

"Because I can't imagine Maura getting into fairy tales or nursery rhymes."

"Oh, yeah," Katie said. "I forgot about that. I guess you're right. She'd think it was childish."

"Besides," Trina continued, "Sarah could write us a great original skit. She's good at that kind of thing. You should take advantage of everyone's special talent."

"You're right," Katie said again. "Boy, Trina, you think of everything!"

By now, Katie's legs were barely moving. She was lost in thought. "You know, there's a girl in cabin eight who's a real actress. I mean, she's been in TV commercials. I hope she's a blue. She'd be great in a skit."

Trina was still thinking about the skits too. "Katie . . . I don't have to be in the skit, do I?"

"Not if you don't want to," Katie responded quickly. "You don't have to do anything you don't want to do. I promise."

"Thanks," Trina said in relief. "It's just the silly stuff I don't like very much. Or doing things where everyone's looking at me."

"But what about gymnastics?" Katie asked

anxiously. "You're so good at tumbling and the balance beam."

"Oh, I don't mind that. It's funny. When I'm doing gymnastics, I don't care if people are watching. I guess it's because I'm concentrating so hard, I forget about them."

"Good," Katie said with satisfaction. "Because you're going to be the star in gymnastics for the blues."

"Megan's good in gymnastics too," Trina reminded her. "Particularly on the parallel bars."

Katie nodded. "Between the two of you, we'll definitely win gymnastics. What else would you want to do?"

Trina thought about that. "Oh, I like relays, and horseback riding, and sailing."

"You got it!" Katie announced.

Trina smiled happily. Last year's captain had put her in lots of activities she didn't like. It was going to be so different this year with Katie as captain!

Darrell blew his whistle, ending their kicking exercise. He didn't look very pleased. "That was terrible! I don't know what's the matter with you kids today. Nobody's concentrating."

"Can we have some races?" somebody asked.

A chorus of voices echoed her request. Darrell looked puzzled by this sudden enthusiasm for racing. But Trina understood. Swimming relays were a big part of color wars, and everyone wanted to build up speed.

Darrell agreed, and the rest of the period was taken up with races. By the time they got out of the pool, they were all exhausted.

"I just had another idea," Katie said to Trina as she dried off with a towel. "Would you like to be my assistant captain?"

Trina was startled. "But color war teams don't have assistant captains."

"Well, it could be unofficial. And I don't think there's any rule that says we *can't* have assistant captains. That way, I could ask for your advice on everything."

"But you can do that anyway!" Trina said. "I don't have to be the assistant captain."

Katie nodded, but she looked a little disturbed. "I was just remembering . . . you know that captain we had last year? Remember when she made that big plan for the sing and nobody liked it? And we all ganged up on her?"

Trina remembered clearly. As she recalled, Katie was the leader of the rebellion.

"Well, I don't want that to happen to me," Katie said. "And I figured, if you were the assistant captain, I'd always have somebody to take my side. You know, stand up for me."

Trina looked at her seriously. "I don't have to be assistant captain to be on your side, Katie. I'm your best friend, remember?"

Katie's face shone with pleasure. "Thanks, Trina."

Sarah and Megan joined them, and they started

back toward the cabin to change clothes. "I was talking to those girls in cabin seven," Megan bubbled, "and they all want to be blues!"

Katie struck a preening pose. "I guess they know that with me as captain, it's going to be the best team."

Sarah grinned. "Actually, I think it's just because they don't want to be on Maura's team."

"Except Erin," Megan murmured.

"What do you mean?" Trina asked.

"Look."

Trina turned and saw Erin back behind them. She had paused to talk to Maura and two other older girls headed toward the pool.

"Just because she's talking to her doesn't mean she wants to be on her team," Trina pointed out.

Katie spoke suddenly. "I almost wish she *would* get red."

"Katie!" Megan and Sarah said together in shocked tones.

"Well, think about it," Katie persisted. "Can you picture her trying to beat Maura in a relay? She's probably slow down just to let her win!"

"No she wouldn't," Trina said quickly. But even as she spoke, she wondered. Impressing Maura and that crowd was so important to Erin. But surely, she'd never betray her own cabin mates.

It seemed like all anyone talked about that day was color war. In arts and crafts, Trina was helping Katie work on a dollhouse with Justin, a boy from Camp Eagle. This had been Katie's pet proj-

30

ect since the beginning of the summer. Justin was one of the Eagle boys who had stayed at Sunnyside for a while when their camp was being repaired after a fire. He and Katie had become involved in making miniature furniture for the dollhouse, which the camp was going to donate to a hospital.

"We've got a great chance to win this year," Katie told Justin. "With Megan, we'll definitely win tennis."

"Wait a minute," Justin said. "How do you know for sure Megan's going to be on your team?"

"Cabin six girls have always been blue," Katie said. "It's like a tradition, practically."

"How do you find out what color you are?" Justin asked.

"It's different every year," Trina explained. "And you never know when it's going to happen. One year, we went to breakfast, and the napkins we got were either red or blue."

Justin thought about this. "So it was just a coincidence that all you guys in cabin six got blue."

Trina and Katie looked at each other and shrugged. "Yeah, I guess it could have been," Katie said.

"I just had this funny idea," Justin remarked as he carefully glued a leg to a tiny chair. "What if all the girls who voted for Katie get red, and all the friends of the other girl get blue?"

"It couldn't happen," Katie said firmly.

"Why not?"

"Because—because there would be a revolution!"

"And Katie would start it!" Trina added, laughing.

"Hey, Katie!" Justin exclaimed. "Watch what you're doing!"

Katie looked at the little chair she was holding. She'd just glued a fifth leg on. "Oops! Sorry. I guess I just don't have my mind on this." She sighed. "I wish breakout would happen. Then we could really get started. I can't wait for the first team meeting!"

"You know, I was thinking," Trina said. "At that first meeting, we ought to bring cards for everyone to put down their names and what they're good at, like running or swimming. Then you and I could organize the cards and assign everyone to competitions."

"That's a great idea!" Katie exclaimed. "Trina, you're brilliant!"

Trina beamed. She didn't need to be an assistant captain, officially or unofficially. As long as she and Katie were in this together, the blues would be triumphant!

The next morning, Trina woke up early before anyone else. Still groggy, she got out of bed and started toward the bathroom. On the way, she glanced at Megan, still sleeping. And her eyebrows shot up. On Megan's forehead there was a splotch of blue paint.

Trina hugged herself in glee. Carolyn must have done this while they were sleeping!

"Megan," she whispered urgently. "Wake up!"

Megan half opened her eyes. "Huh?"

Behind her, Trina heard Katie stir. Then Katie must have seen what Trina was looking at, because there was a sudden shriek. "It's breakout!"

Sarah sat up on her upper bunk, and now Trina could see the blue splotch on her forehead too. Trina ran over to the single bed where Erin was still sleeping, her face buried in her pillow. Trina touched her shoulder gently. "Erin!"

Sleepily, Erin turned over. Trina clapped a hand to her mouth. Erin had a splotch on her forehead too. But it was red.

Trina whirled around and faced the others. "Guys! Look at Erin!"

But they didn't. They were all looking at her. And their expressions were stunned.

Trina stared back at them. And then a shiver went through her. A horrible thought entered her mind. But it couldn't be. This wouldn't happen to her. Somehow, she forced herself to walk over to the mirror.

"No," she breathed. It was a mistake. It was some kind of terrible mistake. She blinked, rubbed her eyes, and looked again.

But the paint on her own forehead hadn't changed color. It was still red.

Chapter 4

Idiotic

Lots of campers were still proudly wearing their splotches at breakfast. Trina had scrubbed hers off. She still couldn't believe this had happened to her.

"Girls, you've all got your colors," Ms. Winkle announced. "And I know you can't wait to get started! You'll be having your first team meetings tonight after dinner. The blues will meet here in the dining hall, and the reds can meet in the activities hall."

It seemed to Trina that meetings were already taking place. Miserably, she watched all during breakfast as girls ran up to Katie and proudly displayed the blue paint on their foreheads. At the other end of the dining hall, she could see campers with red splotches gathering around Maura. Erin had rushed over there as soon as she'd finished breakfast. There was total commotion throughout

35

the room, and everyone looked excited and exhilarated. Everyone but Trina.

She tried every now and then to catch Katie's eye, but her best friend was too busy greeting her new team. So she focused on her uneaten breakfast, and allowed depression to engulf her.

"Trina," Carolyn said gently. "It's not the end of the world."

Trina raised her forlorn eyes. "There must be something I can do. Maybe I could ask Ms. Winkle if I can change."

Sarah looked at her sympathetically. "Trina, you know the rules. No switching colors."

Trina turned beseechingly to Carolyn. "Can't you do something about this?"

Carolyn shook her head. "It was Ms. Winkle's idea to make sure the cabins were split up. She thinks the cabin mates stick together too much, and that this would be a good way to get campers involved with girls in other cabins."

"But it's not fair!" Trina burst out. "How can I be a red when all my friends are blues?"

"Erin's red too," Megan pointed out.

"That's different," Trina said. "Erin doesn't mind being the wrong color." Once again, she tried to catch Katie's eye, and this time she succeeded. She offered Katie a tremulous smile. For a second, Katie's face was a blank. Then she smiled back—but it was a small smile, and sort of awkward, as if she didn't know what to say or do.

Just then, Erin reappeared at the table. Her

eyes were bright. "This is going to be fun!" she enthused. "Maura's got a great team."

Trina stared at her, aghast. How could she say such a thing, right here, in front of everyone? And how could she possibly be so happy about this?

Katie didn't look too thrilled with Erin's attitude either. There was no mistaking the hostility in her expression. It made Trina feel queasy. Was that the way Katie would be looking at her from now on?

Carolyn noticed Katie's expression too. She leaned forward and spoke seriously. "Girls, please try to remember this is supposed to be just a friendly contest. I mean, it's not as if the two teams are actually enemies. I've seen you guys play against each other in softball, and it hasn't changed your relationship."

But color war is different, Trina thought. Color war is—war.

But Carolyn seemed oblivious to this. "You're still going to be friends, even if you're on opposite sides. These are just games! Surely, you're not going to let games interfere with your friendship."

She was talking to all of them, but her words seemed particularly directed at Katie. Trina figured Carolyn must realize that of all of them, Katie took color war most seriously.

Katie didn't say anything to Carolyn. Instead, she leaned closer to Megan, sitting next to her, and whispered something in her ear. Trina watched this with a deepening sadness. Whenever

Katie whispered something, it was usually to Trina.

Erin didn't seem bothered by this at all. "Trina, Maura wants to talk to you."

Trina bit her lip. Then she looked at Katie. Katie shrugged, as if to say go ahead. Slowly, Trina rose and followed Erin to Maura's table.

"You know, you don't have to ask Katie's permission," Erin hissed. Trina just stared straight ahead.

There were still a lot of kids hanging out at the table. They gathered around Maura as if she were a queen, bestowing favors. It was funny about Maura, Trina mused. Lots of kids didn't like her. She was a snob, and she could be really nasty to people. But she was still treated like a leader, like someone important, and kids like Erin looked up to her. Trina couldn't understand that. She would just as soon avoid Maura as much as possible.

But for the next week, she wasn't going to be able to avoid her at all. Not if she was the captain of the team.

Trina recognized other campers with red splotches, and she smiled. But when she faced Maura, that smile faded. Maura's eyes were so beady, and they roamed Trina's face as if Trina were something Maura were considering buying.

"What are you good at?" she asked Trina abruptly.

Trina shrugged. "I'm okay at running, I guess."

"She's great in gymnastics," Erin volunteered

eagerly. "She takes lessons back home. Didn't you win a competition last year, Trina?"

"I came in second," Trina mumbled.

Maura's eyebrows went up, and she nodded approvingly.

One of Maura's friends, Andrea, was looking at Trina and Erin thoughtfully. "You're both in cabin six with Katie Dillon, right?"

When Trina and Erin nodded, Andrea turned to Maura. "Maybe they could do a little spying for us, and find out what Katie's up to. She might start planning some way to sabotage us."

"No!" Trina said, and she was startled to hear how firm her voice was. "We're not going to do any spying. And besides, Katie would never try any mean tricks." It was the kind of thing she wouldn't put past Maura, but Katie? Never. Katie might enjoy a little mischief now and then, but when it came to a serious competition, she would play fair and square.

Andrea and Maura exchanged looks, and Trina could read their expressions. They thought Trina was being very naive.

"Of course, if we just happen to hear anything," Erin began, but Trina fixed her with a hard look.

"We won't hear anything like that," she stated. She remembered Carolyn's words earlier. "This is just a friendly contest. We're not enemies, or anything like that."

Maura studied her fingernails. "Look, Trina, I don't know what color war has been like for you in the past. But this year, the reds are going to win. And you better take that seriously."

She took her eyes away from her fingernails long enough to give Trina a look that made her shiver.

"Wait a minute," Andrea said. "Maybe *she's* planning to spy on us for Katie!"

Trina drew herself up and spoke with dignity. "I would never do anything like that!"

Andrea sniffed. "We'll see."

"She really wouldn't," Erin said. "Trina's not the type."

The whole conversation was bothering Trina. "I've got swimming. I have to go change. I'll see you at the meeting tonight." Turning abruptly, she headed toward the exit.

Erin hurried after her. "Look, Trina, I know it feels weird not to be on the same team with Katie. But it'll be okay. She's not going to hate you or anything like that. I mean, it's not your fault that you got red."

"I know," Trina murmured. Surely, she and Katie were close enough to survive a week's separation. But even so, she wanted very much to talk to her, just to make sure Katie felt the same way.

But it was hard to get Katie alone all day. Everytime Trina saw her, she was surrounded by teammates. She finally caught up with her in the stables during free time. Katie was busy saddling Starfire, her favorite horse.

"Going riding?" Trina asked. It was a dumb question.

"Jumping is one of the color war events," Katie told her. "I want to get some practice."

Trina nodded. She wondered if Maura would put her on the jumping team. She wasn't a great jumper, but she was okay. And it was something she enjoyed.

She didn't mention that to Katie, though. She had more important things on her mind. "Katie . . ."

Katie finished adjusting the stirrups, and turned. "What?"

Trina's words came out in a rush. "We're still going to be friends, right? Even though we're on opposite sides?"

"Of course we're still friends," Katie said promptly. "I'm sorry you're not on my team. But there's nothing we can do about that."

Trina breathed a sigh of relief. She should have known better. Katie was a true, forever friend. She wouldn't let color war come between them.

"It's going to feel strange, though," Katie continued. "Being against each other."

"But it's just games," Trina said quickly. "It's not *that* important."

"Are you kidding?" Katie put a foot into a stirrup and mounted Starfire. She looked down at Trina. "It's *very* important! And the blues are going to win!"

She was smiling as she said that, and Trina smiled back. But she felt funny inside. Katie sounded like she was going to battle. And Trina would be one of the people she'd be fighting.

Maura was ready for battle too. At the reds' meeting, she perched on the edge of a Ping-Pong table, high above the campers sitting on the floor. And she sounded just as determined as Katie did.

"This is war!" she announced. "And we're going to win this war!"

A cheer went up from the group. Maura looked pleased. "We're going to give this everything we've got. And I want everyone to pledge all her loyalty to this team. I don't care if you've got friends who are blues. Not even best friends." She seemed to be looking directly at Trina. "Whoever they are, if they're not reds, they're not your friends. They're our enemies! And we're gonna beat 'em!"

There was another cheer. Then Maura got down to business. "I'm going to announce each competition, and you guys can volunteer for the events you want to enter." She eyed them sternly. "Don't volunteer unless you know for sure that you'd be good at this event. Once I've got all your names, I'll decide who's going to be in what."

Trina noticed some of the younger kids exchange resigned looks. They probably knew Maura was the type who would discriminate against the younger campers.

Andrea stood poised next to Maura, with a tablet and pencil in hand. "Andrea is my second in command," Maura told them. "She's the only person you can take orders from besides me."

She really sounded like a general preparing troops for battle. And Andrea didn't look like a person who was any nicer than Maura.

Briefly, Trina wondered if she could get away without volunteering for anything. But she knew Maura wouldn't allow that. And besides, she *did* want to participate in some of the activities. Katie wouldn't want her to drop out anyway.

So she raised her hand for the running relay. At least that was a group activity, and winning or losing wouldn't be dependent on her.

But when Maura got to gymnastics, she looked pointedly at Trina, so she reluctantly raised her hand for that too. At least, she could honestly keep her hand down for the sing. She knew she couldn't carry a tune.

"Now, who can jump horses?" Maura asked. Only two girls raised their hands, and Maura frowned. "C'mon, we have to have more."

"Trina, you can jump," Erin whispered. "I've seen you!"

"But I'm not that good," Trina whispered back.

She didn't whisper softly enough. "Trina, I'm putting you down for jumping tomorrow," Maura stated. "Now, who can rig a sailboat?"

"I can," Erin offered. Trina looked at her in surprise. She knew for a fact that Erin was all thumbs when it came to rigging sailboats. "If Trina can help me," Erin added.

Trina rolled her eyes, but she nodded.

Finally, the meeting was over. Trina spent a few minutes talking with some of the other reds.

"This will be great," one girl said happily. "I was getting tired of the same old camp routine every day."

"Yeah, me too," Trina admitted. "It'll be nice having different things to do."

And as she walked back to cabin six with Erin, she realized she was looking forward to color war, a little. It was always exciting, having races and contests every day. But it would be so much nicer if she were doing all these things as a blue.

"Thanks for saying you'd help me with the sailboat," Erin said. "I'd feel awful if I couldn't do anything but the sing!"

"You said before you thought color wars were baby stuff," Trina reminded her.

"I don't think it will be so silly with Maura as captain," Erin replied. "She takes it seriously!"

"So does Katie," Trina noted.

Erin agreed. "And that's going to make this a great color war!"

Trina hoped she was right. They went up the steps to the cabin, and she could hear the others inside, talking and laughing. But the minute she and Erin entered, all talking ceased.

"What's up?" Trina asked, trying to sound casual.

"We're making some plans," Megan started to

say, but Katie shot her a fierce look and she shut up.

"Sorry," Katie said to Trina and Erin. "But it's private blue business."

"Oh," Trina said. "Okay."

Katie had sounded perfectly natural and normal. But Trina couldn't help but feel something was already different between them.

Chapter 5

retarded

Camp Sunnyside seemed to have taken on a whole different mood. There was a new liveliness in the air as the girls went about preparing for the color war. Everyone was in high spirits.

And the spirit was catching. Even though Trina was still disappointed about being on the red team, she found herself getting caught up in the excitement. The next day, as she worked in the activities hall making signs and banners with the other reds, she realized that there were lots of girls she liked on the team. Of course, she would still rather have been making the signs and banners for the blues. But she made an effort to join in the good feelings around her. As long as she stayed away from Maura and her buddies, it wasn't that hard.

It's all just fun and games, she reminded herself. I'm not really in a war against Katie. And she joined two girls, Melissa and Kathy, who were working on a big banner.

"How does it look?" Melissa asked Trina.

Trina examined the white banner with its big red letters. She pressed her lips together to keep from laughing. "I hate to tell you this, but I think you made a spelling mistake."

She could tell that the banner was supposed to read "We're a red hot winning machine." But the girls had left out one of the *n*'s in winning.

Kathy spotted the error too. "Oh no," she groaned. "It looks like 'We're a red hot whining machine'!"

Melissa looked at the banner in dismay. "What are we going to do? Maura's going to *kill* us!"

Trina scrutinized the lettering. "We can fix it," she said. "We can connect the letters, like script, and that way we can squeeze in another *n.*" She took the red marking pen and demonstrated. Soon the other two girls were working along with her.

They had just about finished when Maura came by, acting once again like a general overseeing her troops. Naturally, she didn't compliment them on their work, but at least she didn't criticize it either.

"That's okay," was all she said. "We need to come up with more slogans for the posters. Any ideas?"

"How about 'Red's at the head'?" Melissa suggested.

Maura gave her a look which made it clear she thought that was really stupid. "That stinks," she said bluntly. Poor Melissa lowered her head. Trina wanted to defend her, even though personally she didn't think it was a great slogan either. But Maura's attitude really annoyed her.

Kathy looked afraid to even offer an idea. But Trina wasn't about to let Maura intimidate her. "How about 'Red knocks 'em dead'?"

At least Maura didn't make a face. She just shrugged. "That's okay, I guess." Then she eyed Trina sternly. "I hope you're ready for the jumping competition. You'd better do it right."

Trina's stomach jumped. Somehow, she managed to look Maura in the eye. "It's not only my responsibility. There's four other red riders too."

"I *know* that," Maura said scornfully. "But I'm just warning you, you'd better give it all you've got."

"I'll try," Trina said quietly. "But a lot depends on which horse you get."

Maura cocked her head thoughtfully. "Which horse is the best jumper?"

"Starfire," Melissa offered.

"I wonder," Maura said, "if there's some way we can fix it so Trina gets Starfire?"

Trina shook her head firmly. "We draw names for horses. There's no way I can be sure to get Starfire."

Maura conceded she was right. "Do you know who's riding for the blues?"

"No," Trina replied. "I guess Katie's riding. She's very good at jumping. But I don't know who else."

"Are you sure you don't know?" Maura asked suspiciously. "Or are you just not telling us?"

Trina gritted her teeth. "I don't know who's riding. Besides, what difference would it make if we knew?"

Maura's eyes were cold as ice. She sneered slightly, and marched away.

"She scares me," Kathy said softly.

Melissa looked nervous too. "Can you imagine how she's going to act if we lose a competition?"

"Look, these are just games," Trina insisted. "You shouldn't get so worried about Maura. After all, what can she do to us?"

Before either of the girls could present possibilities, Maura's loud voice penetrated the room. "I've had a new idea for a slogan. 'Red knocks 'em dead.' I want five more posters with that slogan."

Trina wasn't surprised to hear Maura pass off Trina's idea as her own. It was just the kind of thing Maura would do. But she wasn't going to say anything about it. Even though she kept telling herself she wasn't afraid of Maura, she really didn't want to get on her bad side either.

"I better go get ready for riding," she told Melissa and Kathy. "I'll see you at the stables."

"Good luck," they chorused.

Trina ran back to cabin six to change into her riding clothes. At first she thought the cabin was empty. Then Katie emerged from the bathroom.

Trina tried to act like everything was normal

between them. "Hi. Are you going to be jump-ing?"

Katie nodded. "You too?"

"Yeah." Trina opened the drawer under her bed and pulled out her riding pants. Katie opened the other drawer and got hers.

"Listen, Trina," Katie said slowly, "there's something I want to ask you." Her tone had that just-between-us-best-friends sound.

Trina looked at her eagerly. "What?"

"Is Maura planning any nasty tricks on the blues?"

Trina struggled into her tight riding pants. "Not that I know of."

She sensed Katie watching her carefully. "You'd tell me if you heard about anything, wouldn't you?" Katie asked.

Trina busied herself pulling her riding boots out from under the bed. "I wouldn't let her pull any tricks. At least, I'd try to stop her."

"But you'd tell me about it, right?" Katie pressed.

Trina felt uncomfortable. "Um, do you think we should polish our boots? I guess it wouldn't make any difference to the judges. I mean, all they care about is whether or not we clear the fences, right?" She hoped changing the subject would get Katie to stop asking her about Maura. It didn't work.

She raised her eyes to find Katie staring at her,

hands on her hips. "C'mon, Trina. Are you my best friend or not?"

"Of course I'm your best friend!"

"Then you'd tell me if you knew the reds were planning to sabotage the blues." Katie's eyes narrowed. "Unless you've decided to go along with them."

Trina was startled. "Katie, you know I would never go along with any mean tricks! You're not planning anything against the reds, are you?"

Katie sat down on Megan's bed and began tugging her boots on. "No. But I guess I couldn't tell you if I was planning anything. You'd probably go right back and tell Maura."

"Katie! I wouldn't do that!" Or would she? After all, she was a red. Wouldn't it be her responsibility to report any schemes she heard about? On the other hand, she would never do anything to hurt Katie.

She felt very confused. "Katie, this is supposed to be fun. We're not really at war!"

Katie stood up and looked at her evenly. "I just want to know whose side you're on."

Trina got up too, and faced her. "Well, I'm on the red team. But I'm your best friend."

Katie didn't say anything. She grabbed her riding hat and walked out of the cabin. Trina stared after her. Why was Katie acting so cold? Trina had only told the truth!

Well, she couldn't hang around here and worry

about it. Quickly, she pulled on her other boot, got her hat, and hurried out.

The riding ring was right by the stables. Five fences of different heights had been set up in the ring. Around the area, all the campers were gathering. On one side of the ring, they held signs reading "Rah red," on the other side "Blue's best," and other slogans showing the team they were supporting.

Trina spotted Katie and the other girls in riding clothes grouped together by one of the counselors, and she ran over to join them.

The counselor gave them a blue or red ribbon to tie around their necks. That was so the judges could identify which team they were on. Then she gave them their instructions. "You'll each draw the name of your horse from this box. Then, one at a time, you'll take your horse around the ring. Whichever team clears the most fences will be declared the winner of this competition."

The girls eagerly stuck their hands in the box. Trina took the first slip of paper she touched. Unfolding it, her eyes lit up. Starfire! She shouldn't have any trouble at all clearing the fences.

She started toward the stable to saddle the horse. Glancing behind, she saw Katie, walking more slowly. Her face was crestfallen. "Who did you get?" Trina asked.

At first, she didn't think Katie was going to bother answering her. Then she made a face. "Misty," she mumbled.

Trina immediately felt sorry for her. Misty was so lazy. Katie would barely be able to get her to trot.

"Who did you get?" Katie asked.

Trina hoped she didn't sound like she was bragging. "Starfire."

"Lucky you," Katie said enviously. As the other girls filed past them and went into the stables, Katie suddenly pulled Trina aside.

"Trina," she whispered urgently, "trade with me!"

Trina was so taken aback she couldn't even respond.

"This means so much to me," Katie went on, "and you're my best friend. You don't even care all that much about winning. And I do!"

Even though she was shocked by her suggestion, Trina had to admit Katie was right. It would be a lot more fun to jump with Starfire than Misty, but Trina wasn't dying to win the way Katie was. At least, she wouldn't be particularly upset if she lost—and Katie would be.

"Please, Trina?" Katie's eyes were pleading.

"But . . . wouldn't that be like cheating?"

Katie shook her head. "It was just luck that you got Starfire. I never heard of any rule that says you can't trade horses."

Trina debated. If she did let Katie have Starfire, then Katie wouldn't be so cold to her. It was worth doing to save a friendship.

"Okay," she relented. She glanced around to

make sure no one was watching, and traded slips of paper with Katie. The gratitude on Katie's face made it all worthwhile.

"Thanks, Trina. You're a real friend!"

The girls ran into the stable, and Trina went to Misty's stall. Quickly, she saddled her up, and checked to make sure the girth was tight. Then she took the reins and led Misty out of the stable.

The counselor lined up the competitors. Trina was second, after a girl wearing a blue ribbon. Behind her, she could see that Katie and Starfire were last.

Trina stood at the horse's left shoulder, her back to its tail, and gathered the reins in her left hand. She placed her left foot into the stirrup, and with her left hand on the mane, she swung her right leg off the ground and mounted.

Misty barely stirred during this process. She was probably half asleep, Trina thought.

All around the ring, the campers were yelling and cheering. And when Ms. Winkle blew her whistle, the crowd started roaring. The first girl took off.

Trina watched her. The horse looked lively enough, but the girl was holding the reins too tightly, and her position wasn't very good—she was leaning too far back. Still, she managed to clear three fences, knocking over only two, which wasn't too bad. Trina hoped she could do as well, though she doubted it. Dismally, she recalled jumping Starfire. That horse sailed across fences effortlessly.

But she was determined to try her best with Misty. Somehow, she managed to coax the horse into a decent trot. As she approached the first fence, she leaned forward slightly and allowed Misty to lower her head so she could see and judge the jump. As Misty went into the jump, Trina remembered to keep her seat close to the saddle, bend forward from the hips, and keep her back straight.

And it worked! Misty actually cleared the fence. Dimly, Trina was aware of the crowd yelling, but she concentrated on keeping Misty going. The horse slowed down a bit, as if she were surprised at her own success. And despite Trina's form, Misty wasn't prepared for the next fence.

She had better luck with the third, but Misty knocked down the fourth. It was as if the horse's attention span just couldn't handle two fences in a row. But she managed to clear the fifth—so at this point, the scores between the reds and blues were tied.

Dismounting, Trina handed the reins to a counselor who took the horse back into the stable. Then she went over to join the campers gathered around the red side of the ring to watch the others.

She was watching the third girl, a blue, clear three fences in a row when Andrea, Maura's friend, came over to her. "You missed two fences," she accused Trina.

As if Trina didn't know that! "Misty's very slow," she explained.

"Oh, it was the horse's fault?" Andrea asked, her voice dripping with sarcasm.

Trina didn't want to get into a fight. Luckily, Melissa joined them. "I thought you did really well. Especially on Misty. She's so lazy."

"Thanks," Trina said, and smiled. She was glad Andrea could hear that.

"It was bad luck getting her," Melissa added.

Trina swallowed, and her smile faded. She turned away from Andrea and watched the jumpers.

The blue who had finished had only knocked down one fence. The red who followed her cleared all five, and now the reds were in the lead. Next to Trina, Andrea started cheering. She gave Trina a meaningful look. And Trina applauded.

The next rider, a blue, cleared all five too, while the red after her knocked down four. Now the blues were leading. But then, after two more riders, the scores were tied again.

By the time it was Katie's turn to ride, the crowd was tense with excitement. If Katie cleared only three fences, the reds would win. If she cleared four, there would be a tie. If she managed to clear all of them, the blues would win.

Even from a distance, Trina could see the grim determination on Katie's face. She wanted to win so much! "Come on, Katie," Trina murmured.

Andrea turned to her sharply. "What did you say?"

"Oh, nothing," Trina said hastily.

Katie took off. She went from a trot to a canter, and easily cleared the first fence. Then she took the second and the third. Trina held her breath. When Katie got over the fourth, a rumble started building among the blues. And when she sailed over the fifth, the rumble turned into a wild scream.

The blues had won the jump! While the reds groaned, Trina tried not to let her face show the pleasure she felt. It wasn't that she was glad they'd lost—she was just so happy for Katie.

She wandered over to the area where Katie was surrounded by a bunch of her teammates, hugging each other and cheering. And when Katie finally saw her, Trina gave her a big smile. "Congratulations!"

She expected Katie to throw her arms around her. But Katie didn't. In fact, she looked sort of embarrassed. "Thanks," she mumbled.

And then Trina was aware of other faces, other blues, looking at her with less-than-friendly expressions. And with a sinking feeling, Trina realized she was in enemy territory.

"Hey, red, how does it feel to be a loser?" one of the girls jeered.

Trina stepped back and looked at Katie. Surely, Katie would scold her teammate for talking like that to her! But Katie didn't say a word. She just stared at the ground, looking more and more uncomfortable.

"Well, I just wanted to say congratulations," Trina repeated lamely. Then she turned and walked back to the red area.

She wasn't mad at Katie. Poor Katie probably just didn't want her teammates to see that she was best friends with a red, she reasoned. It wouldn't look good.

It didn't look good to Maura either. She was watching Trina carefully when she returned to the group. Erin was with her.

"What were you talking to her about?" Maura demanded.

"I was just congratulating her," Trina said mildly. "That's good sportsmanship."

Maura folded her arms across her chest. "I don't suppose you knocked over those fences on purpose just so your friend's team could win."

Trina was appalled. "I'd never do that!" But she couldn't help wondering what Maura would say if she knew Trina had traded horses with Katie. The thought made her shiver.

"Trina always plays fair," Erin added.

Maura didn't look convinced. "What's your next event?"

Trina thought. "Relay."

Maura nodded, her beady eyes getting smaller and smaller. "Well, you'd better practice your running. I'm going to be keeping my eye on you."

Chapter 6

Pure Stupidly

Trina was humming as she strolled toward the arts and crafts cabin a few days later. She was feeling a lot better about the color war. She hadn't been in any direct competition with Katie since the jumping. And even though she still felt strange cheering on the red side in all the events, Katie hadn't been particularly mean about it.

The reds were a little ahead of the blues now, and she had been worried Katie might take that out on her. But happily, she'd underestimated her friend. Back in the cabin, she was treating Trina almost naturally—not quite like best friends, but not like an enemy either. Once color war was over, things would go back to normal.

She thought about the big relay that afternoon. She was running, but so was just about everyone else. It was one of the activities the entire teams took part in. That was the reason Trina planned to spend her free period in arts and crafts. She wanted to do something quiet and restful before the big race.

She was walking along the path by the woods when something amidst the trees caught her eyes. She squinted to see better. Yes, it was Sarah, sitting alone on a big rock just inside the woods.

Trina wasn't surprised to see her there. Sarah frequently tried to find lonely places where she could read and no one would disturb her. But as Trina peered through the clearing, she could see that Sarah wasn't reading. She didn't even have a book with her. She was just curled up on the rock, her chin in her hands, and she was staring into space.

Quietly, Trina edged through the trees toward her. Now that she was closer, she could see Sarah's face more clearly, and she realized something she hadn't noticed before. Sarah's once-chubby face was definitely thinner. That diet the nutritionist had put her on must be working, Trina thought.

But she noticed something else about Sarah's face too. It was sad.

A twig snapped under Trina's feet, and Sarah looked up. A small smile appeared on her woebegone face. "Hi."

"Hi." Trina climbed onto the rock and sat beside her. "You know, I can really tell you're losing weight now. You look good!"

The compliment didn't improve Sarah's expression. "Thanks. But I'm not going to look so good after tomorrow."

Trina's eyebrows went up. "What do you mean? What's happening tomorrow?"

"The pie eating contest," Sarah said mournfully. "I'll probably end up gaining back all the weight I've lost."

"I thought you weren't going to enter the pie eating contest!"

"I don't *want* to," Sarah replied. "Katie assigned me to it."

"But she knows you're on a diet!" Trina exclaimed.

"She says we need to win this one," Sarah said. "And she knows I can eat a lot, and I can eat fast."

"Just tell her you don't want to do it," Trina said. "She'll understand."

Sarah rolled her eyes. "C'mon, Trina, you know Katie. She'll talk me into it."

Trina sighed. She knew exactly what Sarah meant. When Katie was determined, she could talk a person into just about anything. She remembered when they all first arrived at camp that summer and found out boys from Camp Eagle were going to be staying there for a while. Katie was determined to drive them away, and she got all the girls to join her in a campaign to get rid of them. No one was as enthusiastic about ignoring the boys as Katie was, but they all followed her lead.

63

"You're just going to have to put your foot down," Trina stated. "Tell her you don't want to break your diet, and that's it."

Sarah looked nervous. "She'll be furious at me."

"Only for a little while," Trina assured her. "Then she'll realize that you're right. Besides, there are plenty of other girls she can get to take your place. Eating pies doesn't take that much talent."

"That's true," Sarah admitted.

"Don't let Katie push you around," Trina told her. "She's my best friend, and she's great and all that, but I know how bossy she can be. And once she realizes how much this diet means to you, she'll probably end up apologizing for trying to get you to break it."

Sarah thought about this. "You're absolutely right," she said finally. "I'm acting like a wimp. I don't have to eat pies if I don't want to." She hopped off the rock. "I'm going to tell Katie right now. Thanks, Trina!"

Trina waved as she ran off. She hoped Katie wouldn't give Sarah too hard a time over this. Winning meant an awful lot to Katie. But on the other hand, Trina knew that friends meant a lot to her too.

She got down from the rock and headed over to the arts and crafts cabin. She had a special project she was working on. Every summer, she liked to make little gifts to give her cabin mates when camp ended. This summer, she'd discovered scraps of leather that could be beaded and engraved and made into personalized bookmarks for each girl.

She was working on Katie's that day, and she wanted to make it more special than the others. She sat down at a table, looked over some beads and studs, and tried to decide if she should form Katie's initials from rhinestones. Just then, the subject of her thoughts burst into the cabin.

Trina quickly put her hand holding the bookmark under the table and grinned at Katie. But the grin disappeared as Katie came toward her. Her best friend did not look happy.

She got right to the point. "Did you tell Sarah to drop out of the pie eating contest?"

"I didn't *tell* her—" Trina began, but Katie wouldn't let her explain.

"You're lying! She told me she wanted to drop out, and from what she said I could just tell she'd been talking to you."

"She *did* talk to me," Trina said. "She said she didn't want to do it because of her diet. And I said she should tell you."

"And you talked her into dropping out," Katie finished, her angry eyes flashing. "She's the fastest eater at camp! You were deliberately trying to hurt my team!"

"That's not true!" Trina exclaimed. She wanted to explain how eating the pies would ruin Sarah's diet, but Katie was obviously in no mood for explanations.

"Don't you *ever* interfere with my team's business again!" And with that, Katie stormed out of the cabin.

Trina watched her run out in total dismay. Now what had she done? She'd never seen Katie that angry before. How was she going to make this up to her?

She fingered the strip of leather. She had a feeling a monogrammed bookmark wasn't going to be enough.

All the reds were gathered in the activities hall. In front of them, Maura used a pointer to indicate a map of the camp drawn on a blackboard.

"This is the relay course," she explained. "Each of you will be assigned a place along the route. The first runner will be carrying a red ribbon. She'll pass it to the next runner, who will pass it to the next, and so on. Whatever you do, don't stop to say anything to the girl giving you the ribbon. Just grab it and go!"

Andrea was studying the map. "Look!" she said suddenly. "If the runner who gets the ribbon at this point goes between these two cabins instead of around them, she could save some time and get to the next point faster!"

Trina and Melissa exchanged looks and grimaced. Andrea *would* try to come up with a way to cheat!

Even Maura was shaking her head regretfully. "No, we better not try that. There are going to be

66

counselors posted all along the route, and someone might report us."

How typical of Maura, Trina thought. She didn't care that it was unethical. She only worried about getting caught!

"Now remember, everyone," Maura went on, "this race is worth twenty points. Right now, we're ahead of the blues, but only by ten points. We've got to hold on to our lead!"

The girls gathered around the map to look at the course, and Andrea told them their positions. Trina was given a spot across from the dining hall.

"Okay, everyone, get to your positions," Maura yelled. "And win!"

Trina left the activities hall, and walked up the hill to the dining hall. She went slowly, to conserve her energy. Even so, she was slightly out of breath by the time she got there. The blue team must have been meeting in the dining hall, because they suddenly poured out of that building and dispersed to go off to their positions. But one of them remained. It was Katie.

Trina offered her a tentative smile. To her relief, Katie didn't make a face at her. She didn't smile—but at least she didn't look as angry as she had looked in the arts and crafts cabin. She glanced around, probably checking to make sure none of the other blues were watching her. Then she spoke.

"Sorry I yelled at you about Sarah," she mumbled. "But I still don't think you should have told her to drop out."

"I didn't tell her to drop out," Trina insisted. "She said she didn't want to, and I just said she should tell you."

"You encouraged her," Katie grumbled. "Now I don't know how we can win the pie eating contest. We've got too many girls on my team who are watching their weight."

Trina didn't know what to say. "There's lots of other competitions. Maybe you'll win this relay."

"We have to," Katie said fervently. "We're ten points behind you guys! Oh, Trina, do you know how awful this will be for me if we lose the color war?"

Silently, Trina nodded. Poor Katie. She was really scared. If she lost the color war for the blues, her whole team would be down on her. The other team would jeer her. And Katie would feel horrible.

In the distance, they heard a whistle, followed by a cheer. The relay had started. In just a few minutes, if the girls were running well, their team members would be passing them the ribbons.

They stood there silently, side by side, both looking back over their shoulders for girls carrying red and blue ribbons to appear over the hill. Trina glanced at Katie's face. She looked tense and anxious.

It seemed as if they stood for an hour, instead

of just minutes. And then a girl appeared in the distance. She was waving a red ribbon in the air.

Again, Trina looked at Katie. Now she looked really upset. Already, the reds were ahead.

But just a few paces behind the girl with the red ribbon ran a girl waving a blue one. Both Trina and Katie got into a running stance, holding out arms to grab the ribbons as the girls came by.

Trina's teammate came first. Trina snatched the ribbon and took off. She had only run a few steps when she heard Katie running behind her.

Trina knew she could beat Katie to the next point on the relay course. Her legs were longer, and she was faster. But even though Katie was behind her, she could see her face in her mind—scared, frantic, desperately needing to win. It was so important to her! And maybe Trina shouldn't have encouraged Sarah to drop out of the pie eating contest. Katie was probably right—the blues would lose that one.

Suddenly, Trina felt like she owed Katie something. And she started to slow down.

A moment later Katie passed her. She glanced back over her shoulder at Trina, a look of surprise on her face. She knew Trina was the better runner.

Trina let her get a good lead. Then she started running fast again, before the girl at the next exchange point saw her. She kept her eyes on the road straight ahead. But even so, she caught a glimpse of someone up on the slope watching her. It was their counselor, Carolyn. And she looked puzzled.

Trina realized Carolyn must have seen her slow down and let Katie pass. What if Carolyn said something about it to her? Maybe Trina could make up a story and say that she had a cramp in her leg, or something. No, she was never any good at lying.

By the time she got to the next point, she could see another girl with a blue ribbon already racing down the road. Her own teammate snatched the red ribbon from Trina.

"It took you long enough!" she yelled as she ran off.

Trina went over to the side of the road, sat down, and tried to catch her breath. The blues would probably win now. That would make Katie happy.

Of course, that meant the reds would lose. And they wouldn't be very happy about that. But nobody had to know that it was Trina's fault. Carolyn might say something to Trina, but she certainly wouldn't tell anyone else.

No, Maura and the others would never know why. Only Katie knew for sure. And Katie wouldn't tell.

Chapter 7

They are Rejects

Katie didn't say a word about the relay race, not even to Trina. The blues ended up winning, and now they were ahead of the reds. Katie was ecstatic—at least, she was acting a lot happier.

But she didn't say anything to Trina about what Trina had done until they were on their way back to the cabin after breakfast the next day. Then, when she was sure no one was watching, she gave Trina's hand a quick squeeze. Trina instantly knew it was her way of saying thanks.

Back in cabin six, the girls were hurriedly cleaning up and getting ready for the next event.

"Are you nervous?" Trina asked Megan.

"Who, me? Nervous? Of course not!" But Megan was hopping and bouncing around the cabin as if she'd just swallowed jumping beans.

Sarah looked down from her bunk ladder. "Well, *I'd* be nervous if I was playing a tennis match in front of the entire camp."

Katie actually looked more nervous than Megan. But she spoke with assurance. "Megan can beat anyone at tennis. Whoever the reds have, I'm sure Megan's better."

"It's Julie Phillips," Erin interjected. "And she's really good."

"She *is* good," Trina added. "But I've seen her play, and I don't think she's as good as Megan."

Katie beamed at her. But Erin shot her a furious look. "Trina! Who's side are you on, anyway?"

Trina busied herself retying her shoelaces. She was so sick of hearing people ask her that!

Carolyn came out of her room. "What's happening on the battlefront today?"

"Tennis," Katie replied. "Then there's the sailboat race. And tonight's volleyball."

"Whew!" Carolyn sat down on Trina's bed. "I don't know where you kids get all that energy."

"We're not all doing everything," Megan explained. "For me, it's just tennis. I'm terrible at volleyball, and I can't rig a sailboat."

"Trina, what are you doing?" Sarah asked.

"The sailboat race," Trina replied. She saw the dismay on Katie's face. She knew Trina could rig a sailboat well. "Erin's my partner," she added quickly, and Katie's dismay turned to relief. Erin was notoriously slow with sailboats.

"What else are you doing?" Carolyn asked her.

"That's all," Trina said. "Just sailing."

Katie looked at her in surprise. "You're not playing volleyball?"

Trina had a feeling everyone in the room was surprised. And she couldn't blame them. She was good at volleyball. She was tall and fast, and she could jump high. Everyone in that room had seen her slam balls over the net.

But she knew Katie would be on the volleyball team. And she didn't want to be playing against her. All the campers would be watching, and there was no way she could fake missing a ball right in front of everyone. That was the reason she hadn't signed up to play on the red team. Luckily, Maura didn't know how good she was.

"Why aren't you playing?" Erin demanded.

Trina shrugged. "I just don't want to, that's all."

She gave Katie a sidelong look. Katie gave her an appreciative grin.

Carolyn's eyes were darting back and forth between Katie and Trina, and it was making Trina uncomfortable. She was grateful when Sarah said, "C'mon, let's get to the courts. I want a place up front."

"You guys go on ahead," Carolyn said. "I want to talk to Trina for a moment."

Trina could feel their curious glances as the campers filed out of the cabin. Alone with Carolyn, she forced herself to look directly into the counselor's eyes. Carolyn looked unusually serious.

And she didn't beat around the bush. "Trina, are you letting Katie intimidate you?"

Trina let her eyes stray. "What do you mean?"

"I think you're avoiding activities because you don't want to compete with her. And I saw what happened during the relay race yesterday. You deliberately slowed down so Katie could get ahead of you."

"I . . . uh, had a cramp in my leg . . ." It was no good. She just couldn't lie.

"Did Katie ask you to do that for her?"

"No!" Trina shook her head vehemently. "I just felt bad because I knew how much she wanted to win. So I let her get past me."

Carolyn didn't look convinced. "And she hasn't been trying to get you to perform badly to help her team?"

The image of Starfire crossed her mind. Trina pushed it away. "No. Katie wouldn't do anything like that. She's my best friend at camp." She looked at her watch. "We'd better get to the tennis courts. It's almost time for the game."

Carolyn nodded, and they got up. She put an arm around Trina's shoulder as they left the cabin. "Trina, I know Katie's your friend. And I don't think she'd do anything unkind to you on purpose. But sometimes, when a person wants something very badly, she'll do things she wouldn't do normally. Even to a friend."

Trina shook her head stubbornly. "Not to a best friend."

Carolyn sighed. "Just don't let her pressure you, okay? I know how strong and convincing Katie

74

can be. But you have to stand up to her. Don't let her push you around."

Her words were oddly familiar. And then Trina realized why. That was almost exactly what she had told Sarah yesterday! But of course, in Trina's case it was different. She wasn't sure why—but it was.

The tennis match was just about to start when they arrived at the courts. Leaving Carolyn with the counselors, Trina went to the side of the court where the red team was watching. She found a place by Erin.

The game began, and, like all the others, Trina's head went back and forth as her eyes followed the ball. But she noticed that several times when she looked to her left, Erin was looking to her right—at Trina. And her face was troubled.

"What's the matter?" Trina finally asked her.

"I heard Maura talking about you," Erin said. "She thinks you're trying to keep the red team from winning. Because of Katie."

"That's silly," Trina murmured.

"Then why aren't you volunteering for more activities? Like volleyball or the swimming relay? You didn't even sign up for the tug-of-war!"

"Because I don't *feel* like it," Trina said through clenched teeth. "I did jumping, and the relay race, and I'm doing sailing and gymnastics. That's it."

"Well, we've got a meeting after this game," Erin reminded her. "And I think you should sign up for more things. Or Maura's going to be really angry."

Who cares, Trina thought, but she didn't say anything. She just continued moving her head back and forth and wished that color war would be over.

The match went as she expected it to go. Megan took the entire set easily, and now the blues were way ahead. The mood on Trina's side of the court was glum. Deep inside, Trina was cheering for Megan, but she didn't let it show.

She dreaded the red team meeting. She had a feeling Maura was going to be in a pretty bad mood, and she was right. Trina huddled with Melissa and Kathy while Maura yelled at the whole group.

"You guys are pathetic! You're not even trying! You're letting the blues walk all over you! Well, you better shape up. I don't plan on going down in the history of Sunnyside as captain of a losing team. I want to see some spirit here! This is a war, and we're going to win it!"

The members of the red team exchanged uneasy looks. Trina thought Maura's anger was more likely to produce fear than spirit.

"Now, I'm not too worried about the sailboat race," Maura continued. "We've got some good people on that. But tonight's the volleyball game, and that's going to be rough. I want everyone who's signed up to be on the volleyball team to line up here in front of me."

Girls dragged themselves up from the floor and formed a ragged line. Maura took one look at them and groaned. Trina could understand why. There were a lot of very young girls on the team—and they were short.

Maura's eyes swept the room. "You, you,—and you." Trina's stomach jumped. Maura was pointing at her. "You guys are on the volleyball team." Then she pointed to the three shortest girls in the lineup. "You guys are off."

Trina hurried over to Maura. "I can't play volleyball tonight. I, uh, twisted my ankle yesterday."

She was no better at lying to Maura than she had been to Carolyn. "There's nothing wrong with your ankle," Maura snapped at her.

"C'mon, Trina," Erin pleaded. "You're good at volleyball. And the team needs you!"

Frantically, Trina tried to think of a good excuse. How could she play volleyball? How could she face Katie, right across the net? Could she place herself in the back, maybe, and avoid the ball, and run in the opposite direction when she saw it coming? No, that was impossible. Everyone would be watching her.

"I'm in the sailboat race this afternoon," Trina said. "Isn't that enough?"

"No," Maura said flatly. "Are you in the skit tomorrow?"

"No. But that's because I get stage fright, and I can't memorize lines."

"What about the sing?"

Again, Trina shook her head. "I can't carry a tune."

"But you *can* play volleyball," Maura insisted. "And I want you on that team tonight!"

"I know why you won't play," Erin said suddenly. "You're just afraid Katie will be mad at you."

Trina shot her a hurtful look. How could she say such a thing in front of Maura? Even if it was true . . .

"I knew it!" Maura cried triumphantly. "You want us to lose!"

Trina was on the verge of tears, and she couldn't trust her own voice to answer. She just stared at the floor and shook her head.

Maura looked at her sternly. "Let me tell you something, Trina. Do you think Katie would do the same for you? Hah! She wants to win! And if the roles were reversed, she'd stomp all over you!"

Again, Trina shook her head. "I have to go," she mumbled in a wavering voice. She turned and fled from the room.

They didn't understand. Nobody understood how awful it was to be fighting your best friend. She knew Katie must be feeling just as bad as she felt. That's why Katie was glad Trina wouldn't be on the volleyball team. She didn't want to battle Trina any more than Trina wanted to battle her.

She was passing the arts and crafts cabin when

she heard voices behind her. "Hey, Trina! Wait up!"

Melissa and Kathy were running toward her. "Are you okay?" Melissa asked.

Trina nodded. "I just don't want to play volleyball."

"How come?" Kathy asked.

Trina was tired of making up stories. Besides, she liked these two girls, and she thought they just might understand. "Because my best friend is captain of the blue team. And I don't want to play against her."

Kathy and Melissa looked at each other. Then they both nodded. "Yeah, I'd hate it if Kathy and I were on different teams," Melissa said. "But don't you feel like you should support your own team?"

Trina didn't know what to say. Luckily, just then Sarah and Katie emerged from the arts and crafts cabin. "Hi!" she called to them. "What are you guys doing?"

"We've been working on scenery for our skit," Sarah said excitedly. "Wait'll you see it! We've got—"

"Sarah!" Katie exclaimed. "Don't tell *them!*" Then she turned regretfully to Trina. "Sorry."

"You guys are making scenery?" Melissa's eyes widened, and she turned to Kathy worriedly. "We don't have any scenery for *our* skit."

Katie smiled. "Too bad."

"Well, we have to get back to our cabin," Kathy said. "See you later."

Trina walked with Sarah and Katie back to cabin six. "What kind of a skit are you guys doing?" Katie asked Trina.

"I don't know," Trina said honestly. "I haven't been involved in that."

"What about the sing? What songs are you doing?"

"I don't know," Trina said again. "Look, can we talk about something besides color war?"

Katie acted like she hadn't even heard her. "You're still not playing volleyball, right?"

Trina couldn't help feeling a little annoyed by Katie's persistence. "No! I'm only doing the sailboat races and the gymnastics. I *told* you that before."

Katie looked satisfied. Then she frowned. "You sure you want to be in gymnastics? You could tell Maura you hurt your foot or something."

Now Trina was really getting irritated. And she knew Katie wouldn't let up. "I just remembered something I left at the activities hall," she said in a rush. She turned, and began walking rapidly in the opposite direction.

Somehow, she managed to avoid Katie for the next few hours. At lunch, she sat at the other end of the table with Erin, and allowed Erin to nag her some more about her lack of participation.

"We better do really well in the sailboat race," Erin warned her. Trina sighed. "We" meant

Trina. She knew from experience that Erin wouldn't be much help rigging the boat.

When they got to the lake that afternoon, the sailboats were on the edge of the shore. There were eight of them—four for each team. All along the banks of the lake, campers were gathered, waving their red or blue flags and cheering.

The eight red team girls who were competing gathered around Maura for instructions. She told them which boat each pair would have. Trina and Erin took their position behind the boat Maura had assigned them.

Ms. Winkle blew her whistle, and a roar went up. Trina and Erin went to work.

"Unbag the mainsail," Trina called to Erin. "I'll get the battens." She grabbed the strips of wood, and was just about to insert one into its pocket when she saw something that made her gasp. "Erin! Look at the halyards!"

Erin stared at the ropes. Even with her lack of experience, she knew something was wrong. "There's knots in them!"

Trina couldn't believe it. Tight knots had been tied in all the ropes. There was no way they could raise the sail! And it would take them ages to get those knots out! She stood there helplessly, just staring at them.

Maura and Andrea came running over. "What's the matter?" Maura asked.

Trina didn't have to answer. The older girls spotted the problem right away. "Oh no," Andrea said. "How could that have happened?" She and Maura exchanged glances.

By now, most of the other boats were almost ready to take off. "There's no way we can get those knots untied and catch up," Trina said. She looked at Maura anxiously.

To her surprise, Maura didn't look particularly distressed. She beckoned to a counselor, and then turned back to Trina. "They'll just cancel the competition. It won't count."

"But how did those knots get there?" Erin asked.

Maura looked at her as if she was stupid. "It was sabotage, obviously." A counselor joined them, and Maura explained the situation. The counselor shook her head in disgust. "I can't believe a Sunnyside girl would do something like that." Then she ran down the banks of the lake to tell the others the race was canceled.

"I can't believe it either," Trina said in bewilderment. "Who would tie knots in our ropes?"

Maura gave Trina the same look she'd given Erin. "Can't you guess?"

Trina shook her head, and Maura rolled her eyes in exasperation. "It was Katie!"

"Are you nuts!" Trina exclaimed. "Katie would never do this!" Erin looked at Maura in disbelief too.

"Oh, Trina, you're so naive," Andrea groaned. "Katie would do any rotten nasty thing to help her team."

"No way!" Trina cried out. "Maybe somebody on her team did this, but it wasn't Katie."

Maura smiled sadly and put a hand on Trina's shoulder. "Trina, I *saw* her."

Trina looked at her suspiciously. Why should she believe Maura? She was *famous* for her lies. "I don't believe you," Trina said.

Maura persisted. "I got here early, and I saw her fooling around with this boat. I didn't tell anyone, because Ms. Winkle might end up canceling color war if she knew something like this was going on. But I saw her, with my own eyes. It's like I told you, Trina. She'll stop at nothing."

Trina still didn't believe her. Her eyes searched the crowd for Katie. Now that the sailing race was canceled, kids were drifting away. She finally spotted Katie, huddled with Sarah and Megan and others from her team. She didn't look very upset. Or surprised.

Katie *did* want to win. She wanted to win more than anything. And Trina knew how determined Katie could be when she wanted something. Was it possible? Was Maura telling the truth?

Feelings churned inside her. Disbelief—but also hurt and anger. How could Katie have done this to her? How could she be so quick to sacrifice a friendship?

And then she was furious. If that's all friendship meant to Katie, then Trina had no reason to feel any loyalty toward her.

83

"Maura," she said, "I've decided I'd like to be on the volleyball team after all."

Maura and Andrea gave each other pleased looks. "Great!" Maura said.

"And you can put me down for the swimming relay and the tug-of-war too."

Katie wanted a war. And a war was what she was going to get.

Chapter 8

they are
Fat nerds

Gripping her dinner tray tightly, Trina followed her cabin mates to their usual table. But she didn't sit down. "Erin," she said, just loud enough for everyone to hear, "I don't think we should sit here. Let's go sit with some of our teammates."

"Okay," Erin said agreeably. But the others turned to her with quizzical expressions.

"But cabin six always sits together," Megan protested.

Trina spoke coolly. "We need to discuss strategies for the volleyball game tonight." She couldn't resist a peek at Katie's face. Her former best friend's mouth fell open.

"But I thought you weren't playing!"

"I changed my mind. You see, I want to help my team win."

Erin grinned at her, her face alight with appreciation and admiration. But that wasn't the way

85

the others reacted. They looked just plain shocked. Especially Katie.

As Trina and Erin walked through the dining hall, Trina felt pleased with herself. She thought she'd handled that very well. Somehow, she'd managed to bury the pain she was feeling. In her mind, she'd wrapped herself in a steel cocoon that no feelings could penetrate.

"Did you see the way Katie looked?" Erin whispered. "Little Miss Innocent!"

Trina nodded grimly. Unlike herself, Katie was very good at putting on an act. But she didn't really want to think about Katie. Every time she did, a pain shot through her.

"Can you imagine what Carolyn would say if she knew what Katie did?" Erin asked.

"But we can't tell her," Trina cautioned. "Remember what Maura said. If Carolyn told Ms. Winkle, she'd stop the color war." Funny—just a few hours ago Trina would have been very happy to see the end of color war. Now, she couldn't wait to get back into it. She'd show Katie what a real war could be!

They found Maura with a bunch of teammates at a table, and joined them. They were talking about the volleyball game.

Maura greeted Trina with unusual enthusiasm. "Here's our volleyball star! You're going to win that game for us tonight, aren't you?"

Normally, Trina would say something like "I'll try," or "I hope so." But instead, she said, "yes," with such strong determination that Erin looked startled.

"I'm not a great server," she warned them. "But I'm a good spiker. Whenever I'm near the net, pass me the ball. I can slam it over really hard, and they won't be able to send it back."

"You must have strong arms," one girl said. Trina flexed a muscle.

"Wow!" the girl exclaimed. "You'll be great in the tug-of-war."

Usually, Trina blushed when she got compliments. But this time, she agreed. "I look skinny, but I'm pretty strong. And I get even stronger when I'm angry."

Maura looked at her with approval. "Good. Stay angry!"

"And stay up front at the net, so you won't have to serve," Erin suggested.

Trina gazed at her in exasperation. Erin obviously didn't know any more about volleyball than she did about sailing. "I can't stay at the net. We have to rotate."

"I'm not so sure about that," Maura said thoughtfully. "Maybe we can maneuver it so we can keep you up front and not let anyone notice."

Trina shook her head. "Too many people will be watching. We have to play by the rules."

Andrea grinned wickedly. "Says who?"

"We'll figure something out," Maura said briskly. "Now, is everything ready for the skit tomorrow?"

Erin nodded. "We practiced this afternoon, and everyone knows her lines." She turned to Trina. "It's a really funny skit. It's all about how boys from Camp Eagle declare war on Sunnyside, but the girls win by flirting with them and end up making the boys their slaves."

It didn't sound very funny to Trina, but maybe it was just her mood. The way she was feeling right that minute, nothing struck her as very funny. "Do you have scenery?" she asked.

Maura looked up from her dinner. "Why? Do *they* have scenery?"

Trina bit her lip. No one was supposed to know about the scenery the blues had been working on. But then, this was war. And besides, she had no reason to help the blues out.

She nodded. "Maybe we should make some."

"But there's not enough time!" Erin exclaimed.

Maura and Andrea looked at each other, and some unspoken agreement seemed to be made. "Don't worry about that," Maura said. "Let's talk about the sing tomorrow night. Can you guys think of anything we can do to make it look special?"

"I wish we could wear something different," Erin mused. "With Sunnyside tee shirts and white shorts, we'll look just like the blues."

"I've got an idea," Trina said suddenly. "Everyone must have a plain white tee shirt, right? We could tie-dye them red!"

"What's tie-dye?" another girl asked.

88

"My mother taught me how to do it," Trina said. "You use rubber bands to make knots in the shirts. Then you soak the shirts in dye. They come out with these neat patterns."

"That sounds great!" Maura said. "I'll bet there's some red dye in the arts and crafts cabin."

"But do we have time to do it and have them ready before the sing?" Andrea asked.

"Get everyone to bring their shirts to the volleyball game," Trina said. "And I'll go over to arts and crafts after the game and do them."

"I'll help you," Maura said. "Trina, you're terrific!"

She's certainly changed her attitude toward me, Trina thought. But compliments from Maura didn't make Trina feel much better. Maura wasn't the kind of person she particularly wanted for a friend. But the way things were going—Trina needed all the friends she could get.

It was just her luck. Trina stood at the far end of the net. And directly across her, in front of the other team, was Katie.

Trina could sense Katie looking at her. But she didn't look back. She kept her eyes on the ball and concentrated on hitting it as hard as possible.

She had lots of opportunities. Maura had instructed the other girls to get the ball to Trina. So even when the ball came toward the girl at the other end and she could have sent it back, instead she hit it to the girl next to her who then sent it to Trina. And Trina slammed it into an empty space.

But Katie's team were no slouches when it came to volleyball. They fought back with spirit.

Trina rotated with the others. After two rotations, she was still at the net, but with the next rotation she'd have to go to the back.

The reds were winning thirteen to ten when the next rotation came. But Andrea, who was just behind her, whispered "stay there." And Trina did.

But Katie saw this. And she yelled to the counselor who was acting as referee. "That girl didn't move back!"

Trina winced at hearing herself called "that girl." And she flushed when the counselor sternly ordered her to move to her proper position. On the other side of the net, Katie smirked triumphantly. Trina glared back.

In the back, she wasn't much help to her team. She could pass the ball forward, but the short girls up front kept hitting the net. By the time Trina rotated back up to the net again, the score was thirteen to twelve.

The ball was coming back high, and Trina leaped to hit it. But concentrating on jumping kept her from aiming it well, and it went right into Katie's hands. Katie hit it back fiercely, right back at Trina—and it hit Trina on the side of the head. She wasn't hurt, but she was so stunned she couldn't get it back, and the ball hit the floor.

"She did that on purpose!" Andrea hissed in

Trina's ear. And Trina could believe it. A surge of anger gave her more energy than she ever knew she had. When the next ball came over, she aimed carefully and slammed it between two girls who couldn't reach it in time. The next ball flew over her head. The girl behind Trina stepped back, as if she were going for a long drive across the net. The girls up front on the other side stepped back to prepare.

But the girl behind Trina was faking. She just tapped the ball toward Trina. And Trina spiked it down just over the net—too fast for the other team to rush forward and get it.

The reds had won! On the red side of the gym, a great cheer went up. And suddenly Trina found herself lifted in the air by her teammates. Riding on their shoulders, Trina looked down at Katie.

Katie's eyes were blazing with fury. And this time, Trina didn't look away. She glared right back.

When the celebration settled down, Andrea had a message for Trina. "Maura went over to arts and crafts with the tee shirts. She said for you to meet her there."

But when Trina got to the cabin, it seemed to be empty. She saw the stack of white tee shirts lying on a table, but Maura was nowhere to be seen.

Trina went to the cabinet where dyes were kept, and found a bottle of red. She located a big metal bucket, filled it with water and added the dye.

She pulled a stool over to the table and sat down. She was just beginning to make knots in the tee shirts when Maura suddenly emerged from the storage room. "Oh!" she said in a flustered voice. "I didn't know you were here already."

"What were you doing in there?" Trina asked.

"Oh, um, I was looking for dye. But there wasn't any."

"I found it in the cabinet." Trina looked at her curiously. "Your shirt's all wet."

Maura touched her tee shirt. "Oh, wow, I wonder how that happened. I better go change it. I'll be right back."

She ran out of the cabin, and Trina returned to her knots. As she worked, her thoughts went back to the volleyball game. She had to admit, it had been fun playing to win like that. Even if it did mean Katie had to lose. She would have won the jumping too, if she hadn't given Starfire to Katie. And she could have beaten Katie in the relay, too, if Katie hadn't made her feel so bad. As for the sailboat races—that was the final blow.

Carolyn had been right. Even Maura had been right! Katie was using her. How could she have ever believed they were best friends?

Behind her, she heard the cabin door open. She turned, expecting to see Maura. But it wasn't. It was Katie, followed by two other girls from the blue team.

Protectively, Trina covered the tee shirts, hoping they wouldn't be able to see what she was doing. But they didn't pay any attention to her. Silently, they went to the storage room.

Trina continued with her knots. But she'd barely done one when Katie burst out of the storage room. "You—you creep!" she yelled. "I can't believe you did that!"

Trina stared at her. "What—what are you talking about?"

Katie's face was burning. "How could you do that to me?" The other girls had emerged from the room, and they too were looking at Trina angrily.

Trina was totally bewildered. "How could I do what?"

But Katie didn't tell her. She stormed out of the cabin, with her two teammates closely at her heels.

Trina got off her stool and went to the storage room. Opening the door, she saw what appeared to be stage scenery—big painted cardboard trees. They must have looked nice at one time. But they were soaking wet, the paint smeared and the colors running together. And they were torn, too.

A shiver ran through her as she examined the mess. So that's what Maura had been doing in the storage room.

She heard footsteps behind her, and turned. Maura looked over her shoulder at the destroyed scenery. There was an ugly smirk on her face. "Too bad about their scenery, huh? Well, it serves them right, after what Katie did to your sailboat."

93

Trina looked at her sadly. "You shouldn't have done this, Maura."

"Who says I did it?" Maura asked innocently. "C'mon, let's get these tee shirts done."

Trina followed her back to the table. Like a robot, she went back to tying knots. But inside, her stomach was churning.

She was still mad at Katie. She was still determined to help her team win. But the way it was happening—it was all wrong. Completely, horribly wrong.

Chapter 9

dippy

"I think our skit was better than theirs, don't you?" Erin asked Trina at breakfast. Once again, they were sitting with Maura and other red teammates.

Trina shrugged. The judges had declared the skit competition a tie. Personally, she thought their skit had been pretty confusing, with half the girls pretending to be boys and not doing a very good job at it. The blue team skit was more clever—it was about a bunch of campers getting lost in the woods. But without the scenery trees, it didn't come across very well.

"I'm going to get some more juice," Maura announced, rising from her seat. Naturally, she didn't offer to get anyone else some. As soon as she left, one of the girls turned to Trina.

"Is is true you poured water over their scenery and ruined it?" she asked, half in shock and half in admiration.

"No," Trina said shortly. "Somebody did. But it wasn't me."

Carolyn, carrying a breakfast tray and heading toward her usual place, paused by the table. "Hi," she said to Trina and Erin. "You guys are still boycotting the cabin six table, I see." Her tone was teasing, but there was something serious there too.

"Just till color war is over," Erin assured her.

Trina wondered about that. Even when the competitions were finished, would she and Katie ever be able to sit at the same table again? Back in the cabin, they weren't even speaking. Maybe she should look into being reassigned to another cabin.

"Trina, you're really getting into the spirit of this," Carolyn noted. "That was a great volleyball game you played last night."

"Thanks," Trina replied listlessly. She looked up, expecting to see approval in Carolyn's eyes. But instead, her counselor looked curious.

Maura returned with her juice, and when she saw Carolyn standing there, her eyes narrowed. "I think we've got a spy in our midst," she muttered, just loud enough for Carolyn to hear.

Carolyn laughed. "Don't be silly. When are these wars over, anyway?"

"They announce the winner at the camp fire tomorrow night," Erin told her. "Today we've got tug-of-war and swimming relay, and tonight's the sing. Tomorrow's gymnastics and archery. And there are board games all day in the activities hall."

Carolyn smiled and nodded. Maura was still shooting stony looks at her. "Well, see you later," she said, and moved on.

"About the tug-of-war," Maura said, "you know, it's traditional for the team captains to be at the front of the line. But I don't think I should do that. I'd like to give that honor to someone else."

Melissa, sitting next to Trina, whispered in Trina's ear, "She just doesn't want to get rope burns on her hands."

Maura gazed benevolently at Trina. "I'm appointing Trina to be at the front of the line. In honor of her great performance playing volleyball."

Trina could have lived without that great honor. Now she'd be face-to-face with Katie again. But since she was already in this deep, what did it matter? "Okay."

After breakfast, Trina and Erin went back to the cabin for the daily cleanup. Usually, during this routine, the girls chattered and talked about the day's plans. This time, however, everyone made her bed and did her chores in silence. Several times, Trina caught Sarah and Megan sneaking wide-eyed peeks at her. Katie must have told them Trina had ruined their scenery. Trina resisted an urge to shout, "I didn't do it! It was Maura!" Let them think what they want, she decided. After what Katie had done to her sailboat—

let her know that Trina Sandburg couldn't be pushed around anymore. Let her believe that Trina would retaliate.

The tug-of-war was held on the playing field. Campers formed a circle around the two teams, and there was the usual flag-waving and cheering. A long rope lay over a chalk line drawn on the ground. Trina and the other reds formed a line on one side. Katie and her girls did the same on the opposite side of the chalk line.

"Hey!" Katie yelled. "The captains are supposed to head the line."

"That's not a rule," Trina shot back at her. "Maura's letting me take her place."

"Is she your new best friend now?" Katie asked, sneering.

"Maybe," Trina snapped, although the thought of Maura as a best friend made her inwardly shudder.

At the sound of the whistle, the teams lifted the rope. They pulled slowly at first, trying to estimate the strength of the other team. Then Katie's team jerked the rope, and Trina felt it slide a bit between her hands. She gripped it firmly, and pulled.

It forced Katie a tiny step toward the line. Trina watched as Katie clenched her teeth and pulled it back. This time Trina felt herself being drawn forward. She pressed her lips together tightly and tugged.

It went on like this for what seemed like ages,

even though Trina knew it was only minutes. The blues got the reds closer toward the line, then the reds pulled back. "Harder!" Trina hissed over her shoulder at the other girls. They obliged, and now the blues moved toward the line.

She could see that Katie was straining furiously. Her cheeks were red, and her forehead was lined with the efforts of exertion.

Staring at her, Trina's mind filled with memories of better times. She remembered all the giggles and secrets and feelings they had shared. Katie was the only one who knew how Trina really felt about her parents' divorce. Trina knew all about the problems Katie had at home with her two brothers. Suddenly, she felt an almost irresistible urge to throw down the stupid rope, jump across the line, and make up, right there in front of everyone.

These thoughts distracted her, and Katie took advantage of it. Trina found herself tugged toward the line.

And so she concentrated on something else. How Katie had been treating her since color wars began. How she'd tried to make Trina spy for her. How she'd used their friendship to get Trina to trade horses, lose the relay, not play half the games. How she'd tied knots in Trina's sailboat lines.

Fury rose up within her, and with all her strength, she yanked. It was amazing how much power real anger could give a a person. She didn't even know she was so strong.

The force took Katie by surprise. She was jerked toward the line. She struggled to keep from crossing it, but the girl behind her had had enough. She fell against Katie, knocking her over the line so fast and hard Katie tumbled to the ground.

Trina didn't even hear the cheers that went up from the red side. All she was aware of was the fact that Katie didn't bounce back up. She remained on the ground, clutching her ankle.

Trina dropped the rope and ran forward. But Katie was already surrounded by teammates and a couple of counselors. Trina couldn't even see her, until Darrell lifted her in his arms and started carrying her across the field. Even with all the noise around her, Trina could hear Katie moaning.

"Gee, I wouldn't mind falling if Darrell would pick me up," Erin said, casting envious eyes in the direction of the handsome coach.

Trina stared after the figure of the coach with Katie. "I think she's really hurt!"

Maura ran over to her, a big phony grin on her face. "Congratulations! Great job!" She too looked in the direction of the coach. "I have a feeling she won't be in any shape for the swimming relay," she said in satisfaction.

Trina felt sick. Had she really hurt Katie?

"Go put on your bathing suits," Maura in-

structed the group. "And meet at the pool to practice for the relay."

"I can't," Trina said suddenly. "There's something I've got to do." And without even waiting
for Maura's response, she ran off.

Rapidly, she ran to the infirmary. In the waiting area, there wasn't a sign of Katie—only three
younger kids rubbing and scratching at patches of
poison ivy. She must be with the doctor already,
Trina thought. She sat down to wait.

She realized the younger girls were looking at
her. "You played a great volleyball game," one of
them said.

"Thanks," Trina said briefly. She really didn't
feel like getting into a conversation with them.
But they were all eyeing her with such admiration, that she felt compelled to say something.
"Are you on the blue team?"

The girl shook her head. "Red."

Trina was surprised. "I haven't seen you in any
of the games."

Another girl made a face. "That Maura won't
let us do anything important."

Just then, the door to the examining room
opened, and Katie emerged. Her face was pale,
and Trina could see that she was in pain. Her left
ankle was wrapped up, and she was limping.

"What's wrong with it?" Trina blurted out.

Katie glared at her coldly. "It's sprained. I won't
be able to do anything for weeks. Thanks a lot,
Trina. I guess that makes you very happy."

"I'm sorry!" Trina cried out. "I didn't mean to hurt you."

"Sure you didn't," Katie said sarcastically, and limped toward the door. Trina ran after her.

"Really, Katie, I *am* sorry. But you started all this."

"Oh yeah? You were the one who ruined my team's scenery."

"I didn't do that!"

Katie rolled her eyes. "Yeah, sure."

"Well, you tied knots in my sailboat ropes!"

Katie stared at her. "I did *not!*"

"Don't lie, Katie! Maura saw you!"

"Well, Maura's lying."

Of course, Katie would say that. But for one brief moment, looking at Katie, Trina could almost believe she was telling the truth.

But why would Maura lie? *Somebody* tied those knots. And the only person who would do that was somebody who didn't want the reds to win the race.

"Excuse me," Katie said coldly. "I'm going to the pool. Sarah's swimming in the relay, and I want to be there to cheer her." With that, she turned and slowly, painfully limped out of the infirmary.

Trina was supposed to be in the swimming relay. She hurried back to the cabin to change into her suit and practically bumped into Erin coming out. Erin was already in her bathing suit.

"You better hurry," she said in alarm. "It's almost time for the relay."

Trina ran in, stripped off her clothes, and pulled on her suit. When she got back out, Erin was waiting for her.

"C'mon!" she yelled. "We're going to be late." They ran all the way to the pool, and by the time they got there they were both out of breath. The relay was just about to start.

Trina didn't do well. She didn't know if it was because of the dash to the pool that had left her breathless, or if it was because she kept thinking about Katie. When she finished her part, she got out of the pool and watched as Sarah began her part of the race.

Even with everything else on her mind, she couldn't help but feel happy for Sarah. A month ago she couldn't swim at all. But she'd practiced very hard with a boy from Camp Eagle, and it showed. She watched with pride as Sarah beat the girl racing against her.

She wished she could go over to the other side and congratulate her. But she had a strong suspicion she wouldn't be very welcome on the blue side.

The blues won the swimming relay. Trina didn't know where this put the two teams in the overall scores. There were so many competitions going on at the same time that no one knew who was leading at this point.

Trina didn't hang around to hear Maura yell at

them. She started back toward the cabin to change before the others got there.

"Trina! Wait up!"

Trina paused reluctantly and let Erin catch up to her.

"I didn't want to listen to Maura's lecture," Erin confided. "She's really starting to get on my nerves."

Trina was surprised to hear this. Erin had always idolized Maura and that older crowd. "She can be pretty mean."

"No kidding," Erin said fervently. "Trina . . ."

"What?"

"You didn't ruin Katie's scenery, did you?"

Trina groaned. "I told everyone this morning I didn't. Someone did. But it wasn't me."

"I didn't think so," Erin said in satisfaction. "I knew you wouldn't do anything like that. Even after what Katie did to our sailboat."

They walked along in silence for a minute. Then Erin asked, "Who did it? Maura?"

Trina had promised herself she wouldn't tell. After all, Maura *was* their captain. But she couldn't lie. So she kept silent.

Erin took her silence for an answer. "I thought so. That's the kind of thing she would do."

Again, there was silence. But just as they reached the cabin, Erin spoke. "I don't like this. Color war has split us up. And it's creepy."

Trina nodded. "It wasn't like this last year. Or the year before."

"That's because we were all on the same team."
Erin sighed. "Oh well, as soon as all this is over,
we'll go back to being normal."

Trina smiled and nodded. But deep inside, she
doubted it. She had this awful feeling nothing
would ever be the same again.

Chapter 10

dumb

The tie-dyed tee shirts looked great. In the dim light of the camp fire, the intricate designs were much more eye-catching than the plain Sunnyside tee shirts worn by the blue team. Along with the counselors and the other campers who couldn't carry a tune, Trina listened to the blue team's performance. The team had done something really clever. They were singing popular tunes, ones everyone could recognize, but they'd changed the words so they all had something to do with Sunnyside activities.

The red team performance also had a theme. All the songs they sang had something to do with friendship. The presentation wasn't as clever as the blue team's, but the girls sang well. It was while they were singing a particular song about best friends that Trina felt tears forming in her eyes. Luckily, it was dark out, so nobody noticed when those tears trickled down her cheeks.

Melissa slid quietly into a spot next to her. The camp fire must have lit Trina's face, because suddenly Melissa whispered, "Are you okay?"

Trina brushed away the tears and nodded. "I was just thinking about Katie," she murmured. "I don't think we can ever be real friends again. She still thinks I was the one who ruined her scenery."

Melissa was silent for a moment. "I'll bet it was Maura who did it," she said softly. "She's the only one who would do something really mean."

"I'm not so sure about that," Trina said. "I never thought Katie could do anything mean. And then she tied those knots in my boat's lines."

Suddenly Melissa got an odd expression on her face. She bit her lip, and looked distinctly uncomfortable. Trina gazed at her curiously. "What's the matter?"

Melissa seemed to be struggling to make a decision. She glanced around to make sure no one was listening. Then she bent forward and whispered in Trina's ear. "It wasn't Katie who tied those knots. It was Maura."

Trina stared at her, speechless.

"I saw her do it," Melissa continued. "And she said that if I told anyone, she'd kick me out of color war. She even said she'd tell Ms. Winkle I'd done it and have me sent home."

Trina was totally bewildered. "But why would Maura tie knots in a red team sailboat?"

"She wanted you on the volleyball team and the

tug-of-war. She figured if you thought Katie did it, you'd be mad enough to fight her.''

As Melissa's words penetrated, Trina just sat there, stunned. Of course, the more she thought about it, the more sense it made. Maura might be a nasty girl, but she was smart. Her plan had worked.

"Don't say I told you, okay?" Melissa pleaded. "She could still get me into trouble."

Vaguely, Trina nodded. She was angry at Maura, and she felt sorry for timid Melissa. But she had something more important on her mind.

As soon as the sing was over, the campers headed for the refreshment table. Some gathered around the fire to toast marshmallows. Trina went looking for Katie. Frantically, she searched in the darkness.

"Trina."

She spun around. Katie was standing there.

"Hi," Trina said. And then she tried to find the right words. But Katie went first.

"I know it wasn't you who ruined our scenery. Erin told me it was Maura. Why didn't you tell me?"

"Because I didn't think you'd believe me. Besides, I was still mad about the knots."

"But I didn't do that," Katie protested.

"I know," Trina said quietly. "I just found out who did."

"Who?"

"Maura. She wanted me to be mad at you so I'd join in more activities."

The girls stared at each other silently. Then Katie sighed. "I should have known Maura would try to pull something like that."

Trina nodded. "We've been really stupid."

Again, there was a silence. "It's my fault," Katie said suddenly. "I tried to make you feel bad about being on the red team. I just knew how good you'd be in lots of events, and I wanted to win so badly."

She was right. But Trina had to take responsibility too. "I went along with it. I let you have Starfire, and I slowed down in the relay. So it's my fault too."

She wondered who would say the next words first. As it happened, the words left both their lips at the same time.

"I'm sorry."

Katie took a tentative step forward, as if she was about to embrace Trina. But just then, her name was called loudly. "Katie! We need you!"

A group of blue team members were huddled together, beckoning her. "I better go," Katie said.

"Okay," Trina said. "See you later."

Katie turned and started limping away. Then she looked back over her shoulder. "Trina?"

"Yeah?"

Katie sighed, and even in the dim light of the fire Trina could see she looked a little embarrassed. "I still want to win."

110

"I know," Trina said. And then, very softly, so no one else would hear, she whispered, "I hope you do."

The next day was a blur of activities, events, and final competitions. In the activities hall, Ping-Pong balls flew across the tables. There were three-legged races on the playing field. At the pool, divers spun off diving boards, and over on the archery range, arrows whizzed through the air.

In the late afternoon they had gymnastics. There were several girls competing on each team. They'd already been through the vault and the parallel bars, and Trina knew she'd done really well. Even with her natural modesty, she was pretty sure she'd been the best on her team.

Megan had done very well for the blues, too. And as Trina did some warm-up exercises in a corner of the gym, she kept one eye on Megan. They were into the final event now—the balance beam. And she knew this was Megan's weakest event. It required enormous concentration, and that was not one of Megan's best talents.

Megan did a good mount, though, landing with precision on the beam. But as she went through the positions, Trina could see her wobbling. And when she did the turn, she almost fell off. Flapping her arms wildly in the air, she managed to stay on, but points would be deducted.

And her dismount wasn't great either. She had

to take three steps to keep from tripping. There would be points taken off for that too.

Now it was Trina's turn. Mentally, she tuned out the crowd watching her. It was just her and the beam. She focused on the springboard, ran forward, and executed a smooth mount. Once on the beam, she concentrated on steadiness as she went through her moves—high kicks, swift leaps, a graceful turn. She could feel her heart thumping as she poised for the back walkover, but it was like a distant drum. *Nothing* was going to distract her.

And then something did. Not a sight in the gym or a cheer from the crowd—it was a tiny voice inside her. You could miss this easily, the voice said. This is the hardest part, and no one would be surprised if you fell. Katie's team would win, and maybe this event would make her the color war winner. She wants it so much.

But then another voice, a louder voice, answered back. You don't have to prove your friendship this way, it said. If Katie expects you to, then she's not a true friend. And if you intentionally give this away, you're not being a friend either— you're trying to buy a friend. And that's not what it's all about.

So she concentrated fiercely, calculated the distance, and executed her walkover—perfectly. She was aware of an admiring gasp from the crowd, but she didn't let it distract her. She went into her dismount, and landed squarely on both feet.

For a second, she stood there with her arms raised and listened to the crowd roar in approval. And then she ran back to her team. But as she ran, she couldn't help glancing at the blue team.

Katie was grinning at her. And she made a thumbs-up sign.

Chapter 11

Red team is Rediculus
blue team is, Buddy

The night was crystal clear. In the sky, each star was a pinpoint of light, and there was a perfect crescent moon. Its reflection glimmered in the lake. The air was cool, but the big bonfire sent warmth across the lakefront.

On one side of the bonfire, the blue team was gathered. On the other side, with the reds, Trina sat with her arms wrapped around her knees.

The chatter and the giggles ceased when Ms. Winkle blew her whistle. In one hand she held a trophy. In the silence that followed Trina thought she could actually hear the ripples in the lake.

"It's been an exciting and successful color war," Ms. Winkle said, smiling. "You've all played beautifully. And as always, you behaved like Sunnyside girls—no tricks, no pranks, just honest and friendly competition."

115

Trina couldn't resist a sidelong glance at Maura. Neither could several others on her team. But Maura was oblivious to it. Her rapt attention was focused on Ms. Winkle, and her face was completely innocent. Trina shook her head sadly. Why did there always have to be someone like her around?

Ms. Winkle went on and on about the spirit of Sunnyside, and the crowd began to stir restlessly. Finally, she got to the point.

"Of course, there are no losers at Sunnyside. But as in all competition, there is one team which excels, and I will now announce that team. The winner of this summer's Sunnyside color war is . . ." As usual, she paused dramatically, holding on to the suspense as long as possible, "The blue team!"

An incredible shriek went up from that side of the fire. On Trina's side, there were some groans, but they weren't hostile ones. And Trina watched proudly and happily as Katie hobbled toward Ms. Winkle to accept the trophy.

In the spirit of good sportsmanship—and prodded by a few counselors—the red team applauded. Only Maura was making her displeasure very clear. Trina heard her say to Andrea, "If she thinks I'm going to shake her hand, forget it." And Maura got up and stalked away.

Trina jumped up. She'd taken Maura's place in the tug-of-war, and she could take it again now. As much as she disliked calling attention to herself, she forced herself to walk over to Katie, who was clutching the trophy in front of the bonfire and graciously accepting the applause and cheers.

"On behalf of the red team," Trina said loudly and clearly, "I congratulate you for winning the color war." She stuck out her right hand for the traditional handshake.

But Katie had never cared about tradition. She flung her arms around Trina. And Trina had never felt so good about a hug before.

"Best friends?" Katie asked in a whisper.

"Best friends," Trina replied.

Then came the best part, a ritual the camp performed every year at the end of color war. Blocks of lightweight wood were passed around, along with white candles, until each girl had one of each. Counselors passed through the crowd, lighting the candles for the campers.

Like all the others, Trina let drops of wax from her burning candle hit the board, and then, before it could set, fixed the candle to stand up on the board. Then she started toward the water.

"Wait!" Katie said. She dropped her board. Then she let her candle drip on Trina's board, and fixed her candle on the same board next to Trina's.

Trina smiled. Holding the board together, they went to the edge of the water. Other boards were already floating out into the lake, their single candles glowing in the darkness. Trina and Katie knelt down and set their board with its two candles afloat in the water.

And side by side, they watched as the board drifted away, the two candles burning brightly, just like their friendship.

HOWLING GOOD FUN
FROM AVON CAMELOT

Meet the 5th graders of P.S. 13—
the craziest, creepiest kids ever!

THINGS THAT GO BARK IN THE PARK
75786-9/$2.75 US/$3.25 CAN

YUCKERS! 75787-7/$2.75 US/$3.25 CAN

M IS FOR MONSTER
75423-1/$2.75 US/$3.25 CAN

BORN TO HOWL 75425-8/$2.50 US/$3.25 CAN

THERE'S A BATWING IN MY LUNCHBOX
75426-6/$2.75 US/$3.25 CAN

THE PET OF FRANKENSTEIN
75185-2/$2.50 US/$2.50 US/$3.25 CAN

Z IS FOR ZOMBIE 75686-2/$2.75 US/$3.25 CAN

MONSTER MASHERS
75785-0/$2.75 US/$3.25 CAN